"How long has that truck been following us, Stewart?" Penny asked.

He glanced at the rearview mirror as Penny leaned forward to get a better look in the side one. The vehicle was far enough behind them that she couldn't make out the driver. It was a man, though. Looked like he was wearing a hat. Something nagged at her gut.

"He's been there for a while," Stewart said.

"Take a turn—any turn. Let's see if he keeps going."

Stewart smiled faintly. "I doubt we're being followed, Pen."

"Just do it."

Stewart signaled the next turn off the narrow highway, slowed and turned off. There was a sign for a tackle shop and some RV parking. He sped up again, and Penny held her breath, waiting. The truck stopped at the intersection, then slowly turned, hanging back.

"We're being followed, Stewart," she said quietly.

And then just as quickly, the pickup truck behind them suddenly stepped on the gas and thundered toward them...

Patricia Johns is a *Publishers Weekly* bestselling author who writes from Alberta, Canada, where she lives with her husband and son. She writes romances and mysteries set in Amish country that will leave you yearning for a simpler life. You can find her at patriciajohns.com and on social media, where she loves to connect with her readers. Drop by her website and you might find your next read!

Books by Patricia Johns

Love Inspired Suspense

Grave Amish Secrets

Love Inspired

Amish Country Matches

The Amish Matchmaking Dilemma
Their Amish Secret
The Amish Marriage Arrangement
An Amish Mother for His Child
Her Pretend Amish Beau
Amish Sleigh Bells

Redemption's Amish Legacies

The Nanny's Amish Family
A Precious Christmas Gift
Wife on His Doorstep
Snowbound with the Amish Bachelor
Blended Amish Blessings
The Amish Matchmaker's Choice

Visit the Author Profile page
at LoveInspired.com for more titles.

GRAVE AMISH SECRETS

PATRICIA JOHNS

LOVE INSPIRED SUSPENSE
INSPIRATIONAL ROMANCE

LOVE INSPIRED® SUSPENSE
INSPIRATIONAL ROMANCE

ISBN-13: 978-1-335-48403-1

Recycling programs
for this product may
not exist in your area.

Grave Amish Secrets

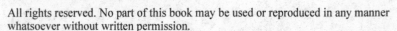

For questions and comments about the quality of this book, please contact us at CustomerService@Harlequin.com.

® is a trademark of Harlequin Enterprises ULC.

Love Inspired
22 Adelaide St. West, 41st Floor
Toronto, Ontario M5H 4E3, Canada
www.LoveInspired.com

Printed in U.S.A.

He brought me to the banqueting house,
and his banner over me was love.
—*Song of Solomon* 2:4

To my husband and son—
you are my favorite part of every day! I love you.

ONE

The winch moaned softly as it wound the cable, slowly drawing up a bag of bones from the depths of the hand-dug well. It was a warm, spring day with the scent of new growth and dark earth permeating a welcome breeze. The beautiful weather and chattering birds overhead were in direct contrast to the somber, grisly scene Detective Penny Moore and her partner, Detective Stewart Jones, were overseeing. But in Penny's experience, investigations into murder seemed to go that way. Life carried on for everyone else—seasons changed, people kept right on living—and it was up to the detective to stop time for the victim and find out who'd killed them.

But this particular investigation was personal. This wasn't just any well. Leaves rustled softly, bringing back fond memories of childhood play in this very thicket. Forbidden play, of course, because the well made the area dangerous for children. But being the daring little rebel that she was, Penny had snuck out here to play quite often when she visited her Amish grandmother in the small, picturesque community of Little Dusseldorf.

In a field beyond the trees, a cow mooed, the sound mingling with that low growl from the working winch that was set up over the now open well, bringing up bag after bag of fresh evidence.

Penny let out a slow breath, trying to distance herself from the ugliness of it all. This was her grandmother Elizabeth Renno's land, which made the discovery of skeletal remains in the long-dry well all the more eerie. This land had been in the family for generations. But considering her personal connection to this case, Penny had been very nearly told to stay clear of the crime scene. She was allowed to be part of the investigation only because she knew the Amish lifestyle and language, which would be pertinent, and the facts that her partner, Detective Stewart Jones, was leading the investigation and she was technically just consulting. But that wasn't about to hold her back.

"Penny—"

Stewart squatted next to the latest remains in the cloth hammock that had come up from the well. He was a tall, well-built man who always dressed impeccably.

A tarp stretched over a section of ground with the evidence lined up on top of it, little markers with numbers on them next to each item that had been dragged from the bottom of that well. The remnants of a black felt hat were an Amish connection to the death, so her guess was that this was a man from her grandmother's community. There were a few fabric fragments of clothing that hadn't completely moldered away over the years—they'd test those in the lab. The collected bones were laid out where they belonged in a human skeleton. So far, both legs were accounted for, as well as most of the spine and ribs, and one full arm.

Penny put a hand on Stewart's shoulder and leaned over to get a better look. In the cloth hammock, there lay a tangle of vertebrae and humerus hanging off a collarbone. But it was the skull that caught her attention. Stewart used a pen to roll it over and he looked up at her.

There was a jagged dent in the back of the skull.

"That looks like a cause of death right there," Stewart said. He ran his gloved finger over the fractured bone.

Penny looked closer. "Yeah, we'll have to wait for the forensic team to call it, but I'm pretty sure that'll be our cause of death."

What could have led to that kind of trauma? There was no obvious blunt instrument in the well, or in the brush around it, that they'd found yet. All the same, this obviously wasn't a recent death, considering that all that remained were bones. The murder weapon would be long gone, but she looked around, trying to imagine the scene that had played out here. About fifty yards beyond was her grandmother's grassy backyard and garden. The home was a big, three-story farmhouse that had started as a single small house about four generations earlier and had been added on to since, story by story, wing by wing. Now it was spacious enough to house a very large family, indeed, although it was only Elizabeth Renno who rattled around inside these days.

Her mind came back to the murder case before her. If the victim died out here instead of the body being transferred after death, the blunt force object could have been a rock, a piece of wood…anything large and heavy. She squatted back down next to the skull, trying to imagine what shaped instrument could have made that fracture.

"Any idea who this might be?" Stewart asked.

She shook her head, and then straightened. "No idea. I've asked my grandmother, and she has no clue, either. She's pretty shaken up about there being a body out here, period."

She'd questioned her grandmother about it repeatedly, but *Mammi* was getting older and a little more confused over the years, and keeping her on track had been difficult. She'd been surprised that her grandmother had allowed a film crew on her land to begin with—the Amish didn't approve of such things—but she'd allowed an art school cinematography group to use her property for a project. All innocent enough, but they'd opened the well to get some terrific shot, and they'd discovered the body.

Penny's mind was already ticking forward with the facts they'd collected so far. The body would have been dumped after death. It went down feetfirst. That blow to the back of the head wouldn't have happened from the fall. She heard Stewart heave out a breath through his nose, and she looked up at him.

Stewart fiddled at the badge on his belt—a nervous habit he had. "So there were no missing Amish men that your grandmother can remember?"

"She's getting more scattered lately," she replied. "But she was clear about that. She said there weren't any. Well, besides my grandfather."

Stewart angled his head to the side and met her gaze.

"He abandoned my grandmother with five kids and left to live an *Englisher* life—" she did the mental math "—about fifty years ago. No, forty-eight years ago. My mother was twelve at the time. She's sixty this year."

"Are you sure he left?" Stewart's eyebrows rose.

Her gaze moved back to the skull. Could this body be her missing grandfather? They were both eyeing the same possibility here, but if this was *Dawdie*—the Amish word for *grandpa*—then what about all the family stories about abandonment and heartbreak?

"At this point, I really hope my grandfather did exactly what *Mammi* said and left the family," Penny said. "My grandfather's leaving affected everyone. His kids all left the Amish faith and went *English*. They struggled to trust anyone after that. Tragically, all of them ended up divorced. Even my dad left me and Mom. History kept repeating itself. If he didn't leave—if he was killed? All that lost faith, all that lost ability to trust—all for nothing."

But Stewart knew about her family's trauma response—stakeouts led to a lot of time to fill, and they'd discussed all of their personal histories. She and Stewart knew each other better than anyone at this point. It's what made them such good partners.

"Did anyone locate him?" Stewart asked. "I know you searched."

"No. I never did find him." Her mother had asked her to look. Sarah had wanted to stare her old man in the face and tell him what his selfishness had done to them. "He might have changed his name unofficially. He might have gone off the grid—Amish guys can do that easily enough. They have the skillset."

Amish families lived without electricity, or modern convenience. Their children attended their own schools, which ended at the eighth grade. They fed their family with subsistence farming and local hunting. A single man without children or a wife could disappear off the grid very easily, or if he wanted some social contact, he could melt into any Amish community without too much question. And he wouldn't stand out. Just another Amish man working as a farmhand or starting up some small business out the back of his house.

"Or, he died." Stewart caught her gaze and held it.

Penny's heart skipped a beat, and she looked over at that dented skull. *Was* that her grandfather's body? Maybe he hadn't abandoned *Mammi* and the kids after all. Maybe he'd been killed.

"This looks like the remnants of leather suspenders," Nick Adams another forensic agent said, sifting through the latest items to come up from the well. "What do you think?"

Nick was a young man with his head shaved to mask some premature balding. He used long tweezers to hold up a leather strap. Penny walked over and took a closer look.

"Yeah, that does," she agreed.

"Considering the clothing, the hat, and the skeletal cues, I'm thinking an Amish man," he said. "All four wisdom teeth have emerged, so he's past the age of eighteen, but he doesn't have much bone loss around the teeth, so not past his late thirties. My guess is closer to thirty-five. We'll know better when we get the remains back to the lab."

A thirty-five-year-old Amish man… She swallowed against a lump in her throat.

"Nick, can you do me a favor?" she said.

"Of course." Nick looked up and met her gaze easily.

"Check this body against the dental records of an Amish man named Caleb Renno."

"Missing local?" Nick asked.

"Yes. My grandfather."

Nick's eyes widened and he gave a curt nod. "I'll let you know as soon we find out one way or another."

"Thanks."

Because if *Dawdie* hadn't walked out on the family and had been murdered instead, she wanted to know it. She wanted her grandmother to know it, too. Maybe it could begin to heal a lifetime of heartbreak, believing her husband simply hadn't loved her enough to stay.

Detective Stewart Jones watched with arms crossed over his chest as the last of the skeletal remains were dredged up from the depths of the well. Penny squatted down in front of the skull, turning it slowly with a ballpoint pen. Her brow was knit, and her lips were pressed together. Was this her grandfather's body? They could do a DNA test against one of his children, but that would take a whole lot longer than checking dental records. Regardless, they'd figure out if this was Caleb Renno or someone else.

For Penny's sake, he hoped it was someone else. Penny looked tough. She had that slim, toned build that betrayed the time she spent in the gym kickboxing, and a no-nonsense look about her. Her dark hair was pulled back into a sleek bun, and she wore a pair of tan slacks and a tweed sport coat that added to her professional charm. But Stew also knew her. Like, he really knew her. They'd been partners for the last three years, and she was tough as nails when it came to her job, but she had some soft spots, too. Like when it came to her family.

Penny stood up.

"Let's go talk to your grandmother," he suggested. "I want to hear her story about your grandfather's disappearance myself."

He was taking lead on this investigation, and it might go absolutely nowhere, but the boss had been clear about how this would run. Stewart was in charge, and he'd have to keep a handle on the case, or they'd both be reassigned. And Penny needed this—if she had to walk away from the body in her grandmother's well, it would drive her crazy. Besides, if this ended up being her grandfather's remains, she'd need Stewart to keep a clear head. She wasn't going to see any of this dispassionately, no matter how much she believed she would.

"Yeah, let's go do that," Penny agreed. "From the clothing, the victim looks Amish to me. *Mammi* might know more than she thinks she does right now. Maybe we can spark her memory."

Stew fell in beside her, his boots crunching over dry sticks and undergrowth as they made their way through the brush toward the tree line beyond, where the lush, green lawn took over. Bugs flew up from the leaves, and he brushed a spiderweb off the sleeve of his gray sport jacket. He wore his dress shirt open at the neck, letting in a cool breeze.

"Now, I need to take the lead when we talk to her," Stewart said. "I want to get her memory of the day your grandfather disappeared."

"You really think it's him?" she asked.

"It's a good chance," he replied. "And if it is, and we tell her, she'll be in shock and will probably remember less. I want to hear her version of events now, and if that does turn out to be your grandfather, I want to hear how she tells it then."

"You're acting like she's a suspect," Penny said. "This is my grandmother. I told you—she was really upset to think there was a body out there. This is my grandmother's land, and that is all."

And Penny would read her grandmother's reactions through a lens of love. That was normal—healthy, even. But her reading of the situation would be far from unbiased.

"Pen, if we don't do this properly, any evidence we do uncover could be jeopardized in court. Do you need me to do this alone?"

She cast him an irritated look. "I know the job, Stewart."

"Good. So then, let's treat this like any other case," he said. "I want an unvarnished telling of your grandfather's disappearance."

"I doubt it's him," she countered.

"Maybe it'll jog loose some more memories from that time period, because right now, he's the only missing person who would match the description. Maybe she'll recall someone else—a visitor from another community, a local farmer who everyone thought left…something."

Penny nodded. "She's losing her faculties, though. You'll have to go gently with her. She was incredibly upset when I talked to her earlier, and sometimes she forgets the year we're in, or what we were talking about."

"Of course."

Stewart had never met Penny's Amish grandmother, but he'd heard plenty of stories about her amazing cooking and her stubborn refusal to leave her Old Order Amish home that didn't even have running water or indoor toilets. And today, he'd get to meet the matriarch of Penny's family. He truly wished it were under different circumstances.

They emerged out of the trees and into the warm June sunlight. He scanned the neat yard. Several law enforcement vehicles were parked along the drive, theirs at the end of the line.

"What's that on our windshield?" Penny veered off and headed up the gravel lane toward their cruiser. A piece of paper was stuck under their windshield wiper, and by the time Stewart caught up to her, she was already reading it.

She passed it over to him wordlessly. The words were handwritten in cursive: *Let sleeping men lie. It was a long time ago. Don't make me hurt you.*

"Not so long ago, it seems." Stewart scanned the area—the only people he could see were all law enforcement, but obviously someone had crept up with their message. He felt a shiver slide down his spine.

"Threatening cops, are they?" Penny shook her head.

"Bold move," Stewart murmured. As if he wouldn't be ready for them now.

"Is this personal—someone leaving the message for you and me specifically?" Penny asked. "Or is it convenient, our car being the last one in line closest to the main road?"

"If it were personal, the one leaving the note would have to know (a) who we were, (b) that we were assigned to the case and (c) who the dead man is. That's a lot for one person to know, and they'd probably have to be law enforcement for that."

The likelihood of a fellow officer leaving a handwritten note that could be examined by handwriting experts was slim to none. No cop was that dumb.

"So…convenient." Penny scanned the area just as he'd been doing, a grim, annoyed look on her face. "Maybe that body is more recent than we think."

Stewart pulled an evidence bag out of his pocket and slid the paper into it. Hopefully, there'd be fingerprints they could run.

"All the same, we're investigating this by the book," Stewart said. "We're following all the leads we've got, starting with your grandmother."

Penny nodded. "Agreed." But her jaw had tensed, and she took another moment to look around them again. Someone had left that note. Had they stayed close enough to see it found?

They headed back up toward the farmhouse, but the back of his neck prickled all the same. The lawn around the house had been recently mown, and a vegetable garden looked like it needed weeding, but it was still growing well. He recognized rows of early cabbage, carrots and peas. He glanced back toward the drive—an officer headed toward his cruiser and got inside.

"How old is your grandmother?" he asked Penny.

"Eighty-three."

"How much of this outdoor work can she even do?" he asked.

"We've been trying to get her to move in with one of us for a while now," Penny replied. "But she's got the Amish community. Different families will take turns helping her out with her yard work and her garden. What's confusing me is why she allowed the film students on her land to begin with. That would be a big no-no around here."

Beyond the vegetable garden stood a wooden outhouse. In the current summer weather, an outhouse wouldn't be a big deal, but how did a woman her age deal with outdoor plumbing in the cold months?

"Come on," Penny said. "I think you'll like her."

Stew had no doubt he would like her, but the personal connection always made an investigation difficult. All the same, Penny knew the Amish community better than anyone else, and even with her personal connection to the case, there was no one else he'd rather be partnered with. They'd worked together long enough that they could read each other's expressions and finish each other's sentences. There were marriages more distanced than he and Penny's detective partnership.

They headed up the side steps, and Penny opened the door and poked her head inside.

"Mammi?" she called, then opened the door all the way and nodded at Stewart to follow her. They headed up six steps and emerged into a bright kitchen. An old woman stood in an apron, her iron gray hair pulled into a bun at the back of her

head and covered with a white prayer *kapp* that was secured in place with three large black hair pins. She was dressed in a blue cape dress, a white apron over the dress and gray running shoes on her feet.

"You must be Elizabeth," Stewart said. The Amish didn't use the titles of *mister* and *missus*. She would go by her first name, and anything else would be considered "fancy," and therefore unacceptable.

"*Yah…*" The old woman squinted at him warily.

"*Mammi*, this is Stewart. He's my work partner. I've told you about him," Penny said.

"Oh, *yah*." Elizabeth nodded. "Stewart. Come in. What have you found out there?"

"Nothing conclusive," Stewart said. "We're just…collecting evidence right now. You did the right thing by calling Penny."

The old woman had gone out to the community phone hut to make the call, since she didn't have a telephone in her home.

"I didn't know what else to do! My neighbor wasn't home." She gestured toward the kitchen table. "Have a seat. Make yourselves comfortable."

"Is that who you normally go to for help?" Stewart asked.

"What's that?" Elizabeth squinted at him.

"The neighbors," he said. "Is that where you go for help normally?"

"*Yah*. They're a good family. They take me to service Sunday with them. They take me grocery shopping, too, but mostly Linda will bring me home what I need when she goes, and I give her the money for it. Her youngest boy is old enough to buy his own buggy now, and Linda says she'll get him to take me on my errands. He's new enough to driving that he likes that. Give it time, though, and he'll lose interest…"

Stewart looked over at Penny and she shrugged.

"*Mammi*, why did you let filmmakers on your property?" Penny said.

"What's that?"

"The filmmakers," she pressed. "Why did you let them come on your property? Your bishop wouldn't like that."

"They were friends of your cousins," Elizabeth replied. "I—" She frowned. "I should have said no, shouldn't I?"

Stewart could see the confused wrinkles on her brow. She looked around the kitchen uncertainly. Penny hadn't been exaggerating her grandmother's mental state.

"Elizabeth, how long has that well been out of use?" Stewart asked.

Elizabeth turned toward him with a patient little smile on her face.

"A long time now. It stopped being reliable when Caleb and I first bought the place. The first thing we did was have a new well dug, and we covered that one over."

"So…before your husband disappeared, then."

"*Yah*, about ten years before."

So whoever had dumped that body in the well had had to uncover it, dump the body and then recover it. That was definitely intentional.

"And Caleb disappeared about fifty years ago?" he asked.

"*Yah*. Caleb left me high and dry with five *kinner* to feed and raise. He walked out on me." The old woman's voice shook. "It was wrong of him, and I can only trust that *Gott* will make him pay for what he did to me. He's out there somewhere. I hope he thinks about us and he regrets what he did."

"Where did he go?" Stewart asked.

She just shook her head. "No idea. Away." She gestured vaguely. "He might be an *Englisher*. He might be driving cars and watching television, for all I know."

"How do you know that he left?" Stewart asked. "Was there any chance there was an accident? That something happened to him?"

"If there was an accident, someone would have told me," she replied. "Plus… I *know*."

She gave him a meaningful nod.

Penny leaned forward. "You never told me this, *Mammi*. How did you know?"

"He—" Elizabeth's eyes misted. "He wanted us to move away from here. He wanted us to go south, to find a new community where there would be more work. You see, we were stone broke. We didn't have a dollar to our names. Caleb lost his job at the mill, and it had gotten so bad that I wasn't even drinking milk anymore. I was saving it for the *kinner*. I asked my sister for help, and she got the community rallied, and they were bringing us food. In fact, they'd all come over that night to bring us what they could part with to help our family in our time of need, and Caleb was furious."

A man with pricked pride—that's what it sounded like to Stewart.

"What was he like when he got mad?" Stewart asked.

"What was he like?" Elizabeth blinked. "He was like an angry man. He stomped around, he said he wouldn't stand by and let them disrespect him like that, and said if I wouldn't go with him to a new community, then he'd go alone."

"So he...packed?" Stewart guessed.

"No. He didn't take a thing with him."

"No extra clothing? No tools? No money?"

"We had no money."

"But he left with his shirt on his back and never came back," Stewart concluded.

"*Yah*, that's what happened." Elizabeth heaved a sigh. "He was upset, and he said that I could have my family and my community, but he was a man and needed his dignity. Apparently, I made him feel like less than a man, and that stung me something fierce. It was an old fight. We both had our backs up. And when he walked out, he wasn't coming back. I knew it. And I was heartbroken for a long time that he did that to me. I couldn't even marry again, because marriage is for life with us Amish. The only way to end those vows is through death."

Penny reached forward and took her grandmother's hand.

"That night he disappeared," Stewart said, "did anyone come to see Caleb specifically? Did anyone talk to him?"

"Oh, lots of people were here," she said. "My parents had come, my sister and her husband, my cousin Ernie—"

Stewart pulled out a pad of paper and started jotting down the names.

"Ernie who?"

"Ernie Schrock. He's passed away now, though."

Stewart made a note next to the name. "Anyone else?"

"The bishop came, and three of the elders," she went on. "The bishop has long since died, too, I'm afraid. And so have two of the elders…" She rattled off some names that he jotted down, putting dots next to the names of the deceased. "Then, there were the *Englishers*, of course."

"Englishers?" He raised his eyebrows. "You had *Englisher* friends?"

"We knew some people outside of our community," Elizabeth said. "There was the veterinarian named Sal. He knew all of us Amish, since he worked our area. And he was very kind. He would bring his son with him sometimes. My husband's best friend was *Englisher*, too."

"And his name?" Stewart asked.

"I didn't offer you a drink," Elizabeth said suddenly. "Do you want coffee?"

She stood up, pushing her chair back with a scrape.

"It's okay," he said.

"Tea, perhaps?" She started toward the big black wooden stove.

"*Mammi*, we're okay," Penny said quietly. "Stewart was asking about the guests."

"Whose?" Elizabeth went to the cupboard. She pulled down a mug. "I'll make coffee."

"*Mammi*, we don't need coffee," Penny said, and she cast Stewart a glance.

"I think I had muffins..." Elizabeth

opened another cupboard, distracted. She put the mug down with a thump.

"Elizabeth, could you tell me about Caleb's *Englisher* best friend?" Stewart said, raising his voice.

Elizabeth froze. "Who, Mike?"

"Yeah, Mike. What's his last name?"

"Mike Miller." Elizabeth nodded. "He owned a hotel in town. The Slumber Inn, it was called. And he and Caleb got along very well. Like two peas in a pod, they were, if one pea was Amish and the other *English*."

They were back on track.

"Did he talk to Caleb?"

"No, he arrived after Caleb had already stormed out," she said. "He was asking for Caleb, and I said I'd tell him that he'd come by. But Caleb never did come back, did he?" Elizabeth opened the cupboard again. "Do I have muffins?"

Stewart flipped his pad of paper shut. This was as much as they'd get out of her today about her husband, it seemed.

"Did anyone ever go missing in this area?" Stewart asked. "Any men who might have disappeared, besides your husband?"

"A couple of teenaged girls go every year," Elizabeth said. "They run off for an *Englisher* life. They want to go to movies and use curling irons."

All that curled hair and movie going. Stewart smiled in response. "Any men that you can remember?"

"No, not just disappearing. Some moved away, and others left the faith, but they do come visit from time to time, you know? You hear of them still."

"Right." He nodded. "Do you have any idea of who that is in your well?"

Elizabeth's gaze met his, focused and sharp. "I'd like to know that, too, Stewart. There's a dead man in my well, and that doesn't sit right with me. He must have family. He must have someone who loved him. He should at least be buried with his kin."

Elizabeth pulled down a plastic bag, and

opened it with tremulous hands. She then proceeded to take out three muffins and set them on a plate. She brought it to the table and put it between him and Penny.

"I knew I had muffins," she said. "Go on, now. Young people need to be eating."

How young did Elizabeth think he was? Stewart was thirty-six—not exactly a growing youth. When Penny took a bran muffin, he took one, too.

As he watched Elizabeth and Penny turn the conversation to the excavation happening out at the old well, he couldn't help but wonder…if the remains belonged to Caleb Renno, how high on the suspect list would his wife Elizabeth fall?

TWO

Penny took a polite bite of the bran muffin, but her mind was still on that note. Someone was watching—someone who knew exactly who was in that well and why.

Someone who knew that Elizabeth was her grandmother? Was Elizabeth in danger? She scanned the kitchen, her gaze stopping at the window. It was cranked open to let some cool air inside. How tightly did these windows lock at night? If someone wanted to break in...a window wasn't going to stop them.

"Has anyone been showing undue interest in the well lately?" Penny asked.

"What is 'undue interest'?"

"Anyone wanting to see it?"

"Just the students who wanted to film out

there. They asked if they could open it. I said they'd best not. It wasn't safe."

"Has anyone come by and asked questions?" Penny pressed.

"Just you."

"Any other officers besides us?" Stewart interjected.

Mammi shook her head.

And who was the dead man? Was that her grandfather's skeleton out there? Was it possible that he hadn't abandoned the family after all? It was hard to imagine— that story having shaped their family the way it had.

Penny remembered her mother telling the story when she was a young teen. *Watch the kind of man you choose—some of them walk out. Good thing your* mammi *was a strong woman, because she just kept raising us kids and keeping us in line. But him leaving—it changed a whole lot.* It had been a cautionary tale about the kinds of men a woman regretted choosing. Some men, in the midst of an argument, just walked out on everyone. And how did a woman even know he'd do it until he did? It was also a warning not to lean on a man too much. Don't need him. Because sometimes they left, and a woman just had to carry on.

Penny's parents had divorced when she was a teenager. Her father hadn't disappeared from her life, but she still remembered the day he tossed his suitcases into the back of his pickup truck and drove off. She'd stood there in the living room window thinking, *Just like* Dawdie *Renno did...* Leaving. It crushed hearts.

While she was pondering this history, the Amish neighbors from next door arrived. They knocked at the side door, and when Elizabeth called a welcome, they came spilling inside. Linda was a middle-aged woman with a kind smile, and she arrived with a cooked meal in a large basket and three of her teenaged children in tow. They got to work without a word—one sweeping, another doing some dishes.

Penny had seen Linda before while visiting her grandmother over the years, and a smile creased her face as she came in to give Penny a hug.

"Hello, dear," Linda said. "It's always nice when you stop by to see your grandmother. But this time—" she pulled back and gave her a sober look "—this time is more serious, I gather."

"Much more serious," Penny agreed. "This is my partner, Detective Stewart Jones."

They murmured a hello and Linda gave him a nod.

"Can you tell me something?" Penny asked. "Can you think of any men, around the age of thirty-five, who have gone missing over the years?"

"Men, thirty-five…" Linda pressed her lips together in thought. "There was a teen-aged boy a few years ago who disappeared and never came back. There was a man in his seventies about thirty years ago. But he was found. He died in a storm. That's not what you're looking for, though. I'm sorry, I can't think of anyone."

"Has anyone been showing interest in my grandmother's property lately?" Penny asked.

"No…" Linda shook her head. "But there's plenty of looky-loos now! Some Amish and some *English*—they've been stopping on the road to watch what's going on. This is the most excitement we've seen in some time."

"Did you notice anyone by the police vehicles?" Penny asked.

"No, not that I saw. Kids?" She turned toward the teenagers. They shrugged and shook their heads.

One of those curious bystanders had left a note. Stewart cleared his throat, and she glanced over at him.

"We should head out," Stewart said. "Thank you for your time, Elizabeth. We'll let you know when we have any news."

They left *Mammi* to the care of her neighbors, who started chatting in Pennsylvania Dutch the minute they stepped out the door. Penny headed down the steps ahead of Stewart.

The sound of that winch filtered out through the trees. The excavation would continue for another day or so. It seemed that when the body fell into the well, there had been some mud at the bottom that had hardened into something close to shale over time. And now they had to chip through it to get all of the evidence. They'd cover the well overnight and leave a few troopers to patrol the area and make sure no one tampered with it.

Penny got into the passenger side of their cruiser, and Stewart started the car. After they got turned around, they stopped at the main road and saw a buggy had reined in and two Amish men were watching the machinery through the trees. Farther down the road, a couple of teenagers in a pickup truck had stopped to watch as well. No one gave their car so much as a second glance.

"So, what's the story about your grandfather's disappearance?" Stewart asked. "Is there anything I don't know yet?"

"That's pretty much it, except my mom said that she remembered *Mammi* and *Dawdie* arguing a lot before he disappeared."

"They didn't try to hide that from the kids, I guess," he said.

"They could try, but kids hear a lot," she replied.

"Did she remember specifics?" he asked. "More than what your grandmother just said, I mean."

"Not that she told me. We could ask her."

He nodded, but didn't answer.

"You're really stuck on my grandfather being the victim," she said.

"Come on, Pen. Pretend this isn't personal," Stewart said. "A man goes missing—the only one to go missing to match the description, at the very least. He and the wife were arguing a lot before he disappeared. People assumed he just left the family, but no one has heard from him since in all those years. He never reached out to children, or old friends, or family members...nothing. Silence. Now, you tell me—is he still alive?"

"I suspect it will be him, too," she admitted. "And if it's him, that body in the well was no accident."

"No, it was most likely a body dumped and hidden."

Someone would have killed him... Someone close to him? Someone who knew about that well, at the very least. But *not Mammi.*

"So let's say it is my grandfather," Penny said. "Then, who is your number-one suspect right now?"

"It's early—"

"Stew, you always have a gut-instinct favorite!" she snapped. "Who?"

But she knew who he'd say.

"Twenty percent of all murder victims are killed by intimate partners," he said. "You know the numbers. And like she said, the only way out of a marriage for the Amish is through death. I'd be starting my investigation with her."

"It's not my grandmother."

Stewart was silent.

"Stew—it's not her."

"If the body is confirmed as your grandfather, we should probably step back." He leaned his head against the headrest. "It might not be your grandmother, but we can't fairly investigate this if she's a suspect."

"When it comes to investigating, I'm the one with the most intimate knowledge of Amish life," she countered. "And do you really think a woman my grandmother's size could bludgeon a man to death, and then lift his body up over the lip of that well and dump him feetfirst? She's not big enough! If it were her, she'd need help. Besides, if she killed him to get out of the marriage, why hide the body? Why tell everyone he'd just gone away? She couldn't move on unless he was well and truly dead! It didn't make life any easier."

"That's a good point," he replied. "Although a lawyer might argue that she may have killed him in a moment of passion, dumped his body with some help from a friend or family member, and then out of guilt, told everyone he'd left her."

"*Mammi* is a stickler for the truth. She insists upon absolute honesty," Penny said. "I used to visit her sometimes when I was young, and lies got a bar of soap in your mouth."

"People can push something way into the back of their minds," he said. "They can almost start over, pretend it never happened."

"And if she'd killed her own husband, would she still be upset about him leaving, hoping that God avenged her for everything she's suffered since he left?" Penny asked. "Trust me, she'd be afraid for her soul if she used God's name in her own defense."

Stewart slowed as they approached a buggy ahead of them. Another car was coming toward them, and he hung back, giving the buggy lots of space.

"Also if we pass this case on to someone else, with her slipping mental faculties, she might incriminate herself by accident," Penny added, "and it wouldn't even be true. We need to do a complete investigation and follow the clues. If they really do lead to *Mammi*, we'll step back, but if we step back before a thorough investigation, at the very least she'll be treated like a top suspect, and I can't imagine how tough that would be for her to endure."

The car passed them and Stewart signaled, then pulled out into the other lane. Penny looked over at the buggy as they crept by—a young family with a man and woman in the front. They stoically kept their gazes straight ahead. The Amish didn't fully trust the *Englishers*, and *Englishers* misread Amish cues all the same. Like this couple—people would assume all sorts of negative motives, but really, they were trying to just mind their own business. And maybe even trying to avoid harassment by the wrong people. The Amish didn't have much to defend themselves with.

"All right," Stewart said, his voice low. "Even if it ends up being your grandfather's remains, we investigate further. But if I call it, we let another team take over and you hire your grandmother a good lawyer."

Penny's heart skipped a beat. There was no way that a lawyer would even be necessary...was there?

"Deal," she said with more confidence than she felt right now.

Stewart glanced toward her, and for a fleeting moment, their gazes met. Good old Stewart—the best partner a woman could ask for out here in the policing trenches. He was a straight shooter with integrity of steel when it came to dotting the i's and crossing the t's in an investigation.

"If it's him—" Stewart's voice stayed low. "If it really is your grandfather in that well, like I suspect, what will this mean to you?"

"You mean, will I grieve?" she asked.

"Yeah. Will this be tough for you? Are you capable of investigating if it's that close to home?"

His dark gaze was compassionate when he looked over at her, then he shifted his attention back onto the road.

"I never met him, Stew," she said. "He disappeared when my mother was a child. He's an ancestor, not a *dawdie*."

"So you'd be okay?"

"My concern would be for *Mammi*. She's the grandmother I know and love."

"Okay." He nodded. "Just checking."

Truth be told, her grandfather abandoning the family had done a number on more than just his children. Penny was gun-shy when it came to relationships, too, and she had enough self-awareness to know it was connected. She had seen too much, and in her experience, a solid friendship lasted far longer than a romance anyway.

"She's innocent," Penny said. "You'll see."

Stewart cast her a wry smile. "When your gut locks down on something, you do tend to be right."

Was it her gut telling her that her grandmother couldn't have killed her husband? Or did she just want to believe it that badly?

"I'm always right." She forced a smile, and this time, she desperately needed to be right. Even if that body in the well belonged to the grandfather she'd never met, *Mammi* Elizabeth needed to be innocent. Penny didn't think she could handle any more family betrayals.

"Stewart, how long has that truck been following us?" Penny asked, peering into her side mirror.

Stewart looked in the rearview as Penny leaned forward to get a better look in the side mirror. The vehicle was far enough behind them that she couldn't make out the driver. It was a man, though. Looked like he was wearing a hat. Something nagged at her gut.

"He's been there for a while," Stewart said.

"Take a turn—any turn. Let's see if he keeps going."

Stewart smiled faintly. "I doubt we're being followed, Pen."

"Just do it."

Stewart signaled the next turn off the narrow highway, slowed and turned off. There was a sign for a tackle shop and some RV parking. He sped up again, and Penny held her breath, waiting. The truck stopped at the intersection, then slowly turned, hanging back.

"We're being followed, Stewart," she said quietly.

And then, just as quickly, the pickup truck behind them suddenly stepped on the gas and thundered toward them. Penny squinted, trying to make out any detail she could, but the truck was mud spattered and nondescript. It whipped past them so close that Stewart turned toward the ditch and only managed to stop a few inches shy of it. The truck sailed on—the license plate obscured with mud, and all she could make out was the first letter—*A*. That was next to no help.

"Who do you know who's comfortable blasting past a police vehicle?" Penny asked as Stewart slapped on the lights and siren, and stepped on the gas.

"Call in for backup," Stewart said. "I want that truck!"

They lost the truck, but it was picked up by a speed trap a few miles away. The driver was unemployed and had a chip on his shoulder. Bryce Miller. He was also driving under the influence—just enough to show on a Breathalyzer. He had a short rap sheet—assault from a bar fight, charged with reckless endangerment of his kids when he didn't have them in car seats. There were a few tickets on file for driving infractions, excessive speeding, careless driving and a DUI from last year. This one would get his license taken away.

So, not related to the case—just a local guy bent on making bad choices—but it had gotten under Penny's skin, he could tell. That note, some idiot blasting past them on a back road... It didn't have to be connected to be unsettling.

Stewart pulled into the Troop J, Pennsylvania State Police station along the Lincoln Highway in Lancaster. They both had offices in this building, their home base, and even Stewart had to admit it felt good to be back on friendly turf.

Penny's office had a teetering inbox, an explosion of printed-off memos she affixed to every surface, and a pile of snack food that she kept in her bottom desk drawer. She could probably live for a week in there without having to leave, if absolutely pressed, and Stewart wasn't convinced that she didn't stay the night there sometimes, although she'd never admit to it. She had some framed photos of her and her mother together and a few other family members, as well as a dog that had passed away a few years earlier. It was a mishmash of personal items and work papers, and probably expressed Penny's personality to a T. She didn't have a work/home dividing line. There was just Penny—all work, no play and no balance.

Stewart's office, on the other hand, was neat, organized and professional. He didn't have personal photos anywhere—no friends, family, parents, pets... He figured when he got married he'd put a photo of his wife on his desk, but even that felt like oversharing. His office was so neat that it was once mistaken for an empty space to be used by a visiting detective who was in the area on a case for a couple of weeks. And truth be told, if forced, Stewart could pack up his area in ten minutes flat. But all the same, he'd wondered if maybe he'd streamlined a little too much.

The Troop J building was made of tan brick, and it had always reminded Stewart a little bit of a sprawling churchyard in the building style—two stories, plenty of windows. It just lacked stained glass. And while Stewart still thought fondly of the church he grew up in, he hadn't darkened the door of a house of worship in at least a decade.

Stewart pulled into a spot near the front doors and looked over at Penny.

"Heading home?" he asked hopefully.

"You should know me better than that." Her smiled looked forced, though.

"This is a cold case, Pen," he said. "Whoever it was we pulled out of that well died about fifty years ago. The pickup truck—unrelated. The note? The act of a coward. He didn't stick around. There aren't going to be any fast answers. You're better off resting and coming at this with a clear head."

"I couldn't rest right now," she said. "I'm wound up."

"You might be surprised," he replied.

"Don't try and fix me," she said with a

short laugh. "Or I'll join in your parents' efforts to set you up with any available woman possible."

"You wouldn't." He shot her a grin.

"Do you want to find out?"

Stewart chuckled. "I surrender."

"I just want to catch up on a bit of paperwork," she said. "Then I'll head home and eat something sensible."

"Thanks." He shook his head. That was something he pestered her about a lot. For her lithe, lean look, she ate a lot of junk. "Use an actual pot."

"I can meet you at a fry pan," she replied.

"You can always come by my place and let me cook," he said. "I'm leaning toward turkey soup and sandwiches."

"Tempting, but I'll be fine, Stew," she said. "Quit mother-henning me. I'm fine. I really am."

And that was the problem—he was worried about her. This cold case was way too close to home for her, and if he was going to be strictly professional, he should hand this assignment back to their chief right now. But Penny had pleaded for the case and promised that she wouldn't be too closely tied to it. From what he could see, that was bogus.

"All right, all right…" He put his hands up. "See you tomorrow."

Penny hopped out of the cruiser, and squeezed her shoulder bag under one arm as she headed over to the main doors. He didn't wait until she got inside—it was open and she'd be fine. He eased away from the curb and headed back out toward the road.

Stewart drove to his home—a ranch-style bungalow on a side street on the west side of town. He'd recently mowed his lawn in a crisscrossing pattern that hit him in the pleasure center of his brain whenever he looked at it. He had a few flowers along the side of his house with rocks around them to keep the weeds at bay. It was probably the most immaculate, but also the spars-est yard on the street. There were no extras. Who had time to fiddle with seasonal flowers or hedges? Besides the blooms by the house, the only other garden bed in the lawn he'd covered over completely with rocks. His pride and joy was that grass. Period. It was easy to maintain and made him feel like he had something under control.

When he got into the house, he pulled out a Tupperware container of turkey noodle soup he'd made the night before and popped it into the microwave. He grabbed some ham and a crusty roll that he'd picked up at an Amish bakery a few days ago and started putting together a sandwich to go with the soup. He flicked on the TV for some company as he worked.

There was a news story about the last case he worked—a body found behind a false wall in a private home. The people who lived there were renting the place and had only just moved in. The last renter had killed his roommate—a really ugly case, and images of the body and the scared kids from the current resident family came flooding into his mind.

He flicked off the TV channel and took a deep breath. No, he couldn't do this. He was home. This was his refuge away from it all. An old sitcom was playing now, and he could feel his anxiety lowering. This job brought along with it a lot of emotional burden. Once a cop saw something, those images were tattooed into his brain for the rest of his life, but he kept one firm personal rule—there was no work allowed at home. Home was his one safe zone, where he could just enjoy some comfort and let his defenses down.

Stewart's cell phone rang, and he glanced down to see it was his father's number. He picked up the call and turned down the TV, canned laughter lowering to a whisper in the background.

"How are you doing, son?" his father asked.

"Good." Stewart put his cell phone on

speaker and sank into his couch. His back was tight from all the hours in the vehicle that day. "Busy, but productive. You know how it is."

"I'm glad," his father replied. "You know, our church is having a young adults' pot-luck next weekend. We thought you might want to come?"

"Dad, I'm not a young adult. I'm thirty-six." He shook his head.

"Right, right…" he sighed. "Your mother said as much."

"Listen to Mom," he chuckled.

"We both wish you'd come back to church," his father said. "Don't you miss a weekly service at all? I mean, the things you see every day—the things people are capable of doing to each other—don't you ever need something to build you back up again?"

That was a little too timely right now, but church had stopped comforting him lately. There was too much garbage out there, and a warm and cozy sermon didn't cover the half of what he needed. Home was his bastion away from it all, and church was supposed to provide answers—it didn't. He was glad the civilians had something that helped them sleep at night, but it wasn't so easy to achieve for a police detective. Though Lancaster didn't have nearly the number of gruesome crimes of larger cities, it had its fair share of homicides and assaults, as well as other felonies committed by people on the edge of civilized society. Those and vehicular accident scenes left indelible impressions.

"I don't feel like it fits anymore, Dad," he said.

"Maybe a different church," he suggested. "It doesn't have to be ours, but I have to say, there is something special about a congregation that has known you since you were tiny."

He heard the muffled sound of his mother's voice in the background.

"Your mother says that she knows a

woman she wants to introduce you to," he added.

"Her name is Selena, and she's a psychiatrist!" His mother must have leaned close enough to the phone to be heard clearly.

Stewart burst out laughing. "Is that the point we're at—you're throwing shrinks at me now?"

His father laughed, too. "No, no, that sounds worse than it is. But she's recently divorced, and your mother thinks she's both successful and delightful. She might be a good match."

"You guys, I will eventually get married and settle down. I will! But I'm working a tough case right now. It's a cold case from Penny's Amish grandmother's property. I'm going to have my hands full with the case and Penny, and—"

"Poor girl," his father said. "I'm sorry to hear that. That has to be emotional for her."

"Yeah, it is, but Penny's a tough one."

"No woman is that tough, no matter how

much she pretends to be," his mother said. Was he on speaker phone now? He must be. "You should bring Penny by and we'll make you two a nice dinner."

"That wasn't even subtle," Stewart said with a laugh. "But I might take you up on that. We'll be working some long hours. But no showing her baby pictures, or I'll never bring her back."

"Deal," his father said. "We'll take what we can get."

"And Mom and Dad, just so you know, when I do settle down, it's not going to be with someone from my line of work, or someone who works with trauma, or...that sort of thing. Your psychiatrist is out, I'm afraid. I'm going to need someone unsullied by all of this, who can remind me of the good in the world."

There was a pause, then his mother said, "Okay, I'm on it."

"That wasn't a challenge!" he laughed.

But that was his mom. She'd do anything for him, including sleuthing out some available women she thought would be a good match for him. They loved him. He had a supportive, reliable family, and he never took that for granted.

After he'd said his goodbyes and ended the call, Stewart headed back into the kitchen to eat his dinner. He checked his personal email while he munched on his sandwich and finished off a hearty bowl of soup. The TV moved from the sitcom to the news.

He returned to the living room to catch the rest of the top stories. It started with a jewelry store robbery in the middle of a big mall, the suspects still at large. His phone rang again, and he half expected it to be his mother with another potential date for him already dug up and dusted off, but the number was from the office.

He picked up the call.

"Hi, Detective Jones? This is Nick Adams from forensics. I've got an identity for the body we pulled out of the well today. I know you'd rather have us leave you a message for tomorrow, but this one—I'd just feel bad leaving it as a voicemail."

Yeah, no one seemed to fully respect his line between work and home.

"Okay," Stewart said with a sigh. "Who is he?"

"Your partner was right—it's a man named Caleb Renno. Her grandfather, she said. We've got dental records that confirm it."

"Perfect," Stewart said, but his chest felt tight.

"I'd promised Detective Moore that I'd let her know right away when I got the results, but since this is going to be a pretty personal hit, I was wondering how I should handle that."

Nick was right to be careful with this one. Even Stewart wasn't sure what this news would mean to Penny.

"I'll head down to her place," Stewart said. "She should be home by now. I'll tell her myself, face-to-face."

"Thanks," Nick said. "I appreciate that.

It didn't feel right to hit her with that tonight."

"No problem," Stewart said. "I'll take care of it. Hey, how come you're still at work?"

"Just finishing up a few things."

"Don't burn out," Stewart said. "You've got a family waiting for you at home, don't you?"

"Uh…yeah. Erin's at home, but I think she likes the time away from me, honestly."

Stewart had heard a few rumors about there being trouble in paradise at the Adams home, but he didn't like poking into his colleague's personal business. So all he said was, "Well, don't stay late on our account. Have a good night, Nick."

Stewart ended the call, put his dishes into the dishwasher, and stood for a moment in his kitchen. This was it—the report he'd been expecting and dreading in equal measure. The victim was Penny's grandfather, and they were now officially looking for Caleb Renno's murderer.

He grabbed his keys and wallet and headed for the door. This kind of news needed to be delivered gently and in person.

THREE

The sun had set, and the sky was dark by the time Penny stopped by a Mexican fast-food place on the way home. Who was she fooling? She wasn't going to cook tonight. She ordered a burrito and cheesy fries, and the inside of her car smelled delicious as she headed back to her apartment building in the center of Lancaster.

She parked in her underground space, grabbed her shoulder bag and the paper bag with her food in it and headed to the elevator and up to her fourth-floor condo. She loved this flat—her first big adult purchase. People kept asking when she'd upgrade to a house, and she didn't think she ever would. She liked the compact nature of her little two-bedroom unit. She could walk to Central Market from here and to art galleries, concert venues and the theater on Prince Street.

The second bedroom she used for a home office, and there was a generous balcony where she liked to stand with a hot mug of coffee in the morning before she got started with her day.

Penny tossed the food onto the kitchen table and proceeded to hang up her sport jacket. She grabbed a bottle of hot sauce from the fridge and deposited it next to the brown paper bag.

Penny might have been raised with a deep fondness for her Amish grandmother who, in the Pennsylvania Dutch tradition, used lots of lard for flavor, but her real comfort food was something spicy. She and her mom used to try out different Mexican restaurants, and she'd developed a taste for hot sauce.

She stopped at her fish tank in the living room and bent down to look at the five goldfish swimming around in the depths.

"Hello, class," she said softly. "You should probably eat before I do."

She'd jokingly started referring to her "school" of fish, and over time she'd started thinking of them as her own little class of preschoolers. Sometimes they picked on each other, but most of the time, they just swam around with the plastic plants and the pink castle ruins. She put some fish food on the top of the water, and they swam up to gulp the flakes down.

Penny washed her hands and headed back to the table. She unwrapped the burrito, added some extra hot sauce inside and then took a savory bite. It was perfect—beans, meat, rice, guacamole, sour cream and a hit of extraspicy hot sauce. She chewed slowly, then popped a French fry drenched in that hot, processed cheese mixture into her mouth. This was what she needed...

Stewart would be appalled, and she smiled to herself at the thought. She'd work off the extra calories with an early morning run. Not that he ever cared about calories. He was more of a worrier when it came to her simply taking care of herself—resting, sleeping, finding a way to release the stress. And yes, eating like her body was a temple.

She got a text and looked down at it as she chewed. It was Stewart.

I'm coming by. Hope you don't mind. I'll be there in ten minutes.

Her fingertips were currently busy holding her burrito together. She swallowed.

"Hey Siri, tell Stewart that's fine. I'm just having dinner now. You aren't interrupting."

She took another bite, followed by another couple of fries. She was hungrier than she'd thought and she consumed the meal quickly, then washed it down with a glass of juice from the fridge. There—she'd skipped on the soft drink and gone for apple juice instead. That had to count for something. Take that, Stew.

By the time she finished eating, balled up the wrappers and paper bag, and tossed them into the trash, her cell phone rang with the buzzer downstairs. She picked up the call.

"It's me," Stew said, and she pushed the number to release the lock.

Her apartment was relatively clean, but she glanced around all the same, just to be sure. Stewart was a neat freak, and while he'd never criticize her, he had folded laundry and done her dishes before. Granted, she'd been down with the flu at the time, but still.

When she heard a knock, she headed to the door and looked out the peephole. It was Stew, and she opened up.

"Come in," she said, stepping back. "Are you antsy tonight, or something?"

He shut the door behind him, and he held out a paper bakery bag. His expression was grim, though.

"For me?" She accepted the bag, opened it and looked inside. It held a chocolate-covered éclair, the fluffy white filling squeezing out the sides. "Oh, wow, Stew. This must be serious." But she knew by the look on his face, and the éclair in the bag. "You got the results on the body, didn't you?"

"Yeah."

"It's him?"

Stew nodded. "It is. I'm sorry."

Penny exhaled a slow breath, searching inside herself, trying to process precisely what she was feeling. She'd feared this news, but somehow, the anticipation had been worse than the confirmation. It was as if she'd known all along, as soon as they got the call about the bones.

But this did change things… It changed everything!

"So my grandfather didn't leave," she said softly. "He was killed."

The stories she'd been told all her life tumbled through her head. *Some men leave. Some men don't want to stand by you. You'd better be prepared to take care of yourself, because who knows how long a man will stick around?*

Stew eased past her, plucked the bag out of her hand and headed for the kitchen. He came back a moment later with the éclair on a dish. He pointed at the couch, and Penny wordlessly sat down, then accepted the plate.

"This is big," Stewart said.

"Yeah…" she breathed. "I never met him. It's not like I knew him, or had fond memories at all. If anything, I thought the worst of him all my life. He was an example of a man who didn't want to stick around and raise his five kids."

Steward sat down next to her, and she exhaled a deep sigh.

"But if he didn't walk out on his family…" Stewart nudged.

"Then maybe I can stop hating him in absentia," she said. "He was killed. Murdered…"

"By someone who knew him well enough that they knew where the old well was located," Stewart said.

"There's that," she murmured. "And whoever knew him well enough to know about the old well would have watched his widow soldier on by herself, the kids getting angrier and angrier..."

"That's definitely cold," Stew said.

Penny was silent for a moment, considering all of this. What had her husband's apparent desertion done to *Mammi* Elizabeth? She'd been gutted in a unique way. Losing a husband to death, she could have grieved properly, could have even remarried, but believing that her husband had stopped loving her had been worse.

"It might have been a crime of passion," Stewart said. "An argument gone wrong, maybe. The people closest to you tend to know how to hurt you the worst. Maybe they'd argued, said things they didn't mean... A piece of wood...maybe an iron skillet..."

"Stew! You still think it was my grand-mother?" she demanded, tuning into his words.

"I think it's possible. We have to at least examine it."

As bad as it made her feel, he was right, of course. She couldn't avoid the possibility.

"Okay, so let's say she did it," Penny said. "Let's say she did murder him in a frenzy of rage over something stupid he said. How would she have dragged the body out to the old well by herself? And then lifted it high enough to dump it feetfirst into the well? You saw the size of my grandmother. She's currently barely over five feet. In her prime, that would make her at most…five foot four?"

Stewart nodded. "About that."

"How tall are the remains?"

"I think they established a man between five foot ten and six feet," he said. "Yeah, she'd never be able to do it by herself."

"And if he disappeared that night, with

all those people coming to bring food and donations for the family, there was no way she could even rope someone into helping her without a whole lot of witnesses. She was the center of attention. There is no way my grandmother did this."

"I'm inclined to agree," he said. "But we're going to have to eliminate her for the record. We're going to have to talk to all those people who were there that night and see what they recall."

"The ones who are still alive, that is," she said.

They met each other's gaze and she felt some mist in her eyes. Suddenly, this shock to her family wasn't quite so overwhelming. She had someone to help her, support her.

"Thank you for this, Stew."

"You deserve a treat," he said.

"No, I mean...you know how to jump-start my brain and get me thinking more logically. I needed that."

"Hey, what are partners for?" Stew said,

and he cleared his throat. "You also need sugar. Eat that."

He pointed at the eclair, and she lifted it to her lips and took a bite. It tasted even better than it looked, and she tore it carefully in half and handed him the rest.

"Share it with me?" she said.

Stewart smiled and accepted the other half, and they ate in silence. Stewart had a bit of whipped cream in the corner of his mouth, and she didn't mention it. Stew was endearing when he was a little less than perfect.

"We'll have to go visit your grandmother again," he said. "Give her the news."

She nodded. "Yes, absolutely."

"And we have some names of people who were present that night," Stewart said. "Let's start with them tomorrow."

She nodded again. "Like my mother. She was twelve at the time. She remembers it clearly enough to have told me about it over the years. But she might remember something helpful."

"Perfect." Stew licked off his fingers, and then wiped the dab of cream from his face. "And I'll leave soon, but first of all, what do you need to unwind tonight?"

"I don't know…"

"How about *Meet me in St. Louis*?" Stew shot her a rueful grin. "You love Judy Garland."

"Actually, yeah."

How did Stew know her this well? Funny—when her life got flipped upside down, it wasn't family or a close friend who knew what she needed most, but her work partner. What did that say about her work/life balance? Nothing good! Still, she was grateful for him.

The next morning, Stewart and Penny met at the station like they usually did. They had a chat with their boss about the state of this cold case and Sergeant Garcia agreed that given the evidence so far, the likelihood of Penny's grandmother being the killer was incredibly slim, so they were permitted to stay on the case unless the evidence began to point closer to home.

Today, Penny was the one driving since they were heading out of town to the bedroom community of New Holland where her mother lived. *Mammi* Elizabeth needed to be told, but they'd decided to talk with Penny's mother, Sarah, first, since she was closer, and then they could drive out to Amish country. It would save time and fuel. They headed out of the station together and found their shared white state-police cruiser in the lot.

"I got your coffee," she said, gesturing to two large Starbucks cups in the cup holders. "Just the way you like it."

"Thanks." And he meant that. Part of the reason why they made such good partners was that they both put in effort to make their professional relationship as easy as possible. They'd been taking turns getting each other coffee for the last three years, and they knew each other's favorite orders. Hers was double cream and double sugar, and his was with oat milk and two sweeteners. What could he say? He liked the taste.

"Did you talk to your mother last night?" he asked as they pulled onto the road and she stepped on the gas.

"Of course. She called to see what was happening with the body in *Mammi*'s well after you left last night," she replied. "And she's doing her best to remember what she can from that day in hopes that it will help us figure out who killed her father."

"How is she dealing with the news that her dad was killed?" he asked.

"Not well."

That was to be expected. Penny's entire family was going to be shaken up by this, but at least he knew how to handle that.

The drive to New Holland was a pleasant, sunny half hour, and by the time they pulled into the drive in front of Sarah Moore's townhouse, they'd finished their coffees. The curtain in the front window flicked, and Penny looked over at Stewart.

"She's going to be a wreck today," Penny said. "I told her I'd come by this morning. She hated her father for a long time because he left, and now she's found out he didn't leave her at all. He'd been on the family property all that time, and someone killed him. She was pretty overwrought last night, and this will be tough… So just be gentle with her."

"Of course," Stewart said with a frown. "What we need is just her memories of that day. That's all."

Penny looked like she wanted to say more, but she didn't. Instead she nodded and got out of the vehicle. Stewart followed suit and stayed a step behind her as she went up the walk to the front door.

The brick townhouses were at least fifty years old, but they'd been kept up, and Sarah's little front yard was neatly mown with a small flower garden and what looked like an attempt at a sparse vegetable plot, which wasn't flourishing.

The front door opened before they even

reached it and a slim woman with dyed red hair stood in the doorway, an apron worn over jeans and a T-shirt.

"Hi, sweet pea," Sarah said, reaching out to pull Penny into a hug.

Stewart smothered a smile. He'd always liked that little nickname her mother used on her. He'd heard it over the phone a couple of times through the years.

"This must be the elusive Stewart," Sarah said, releasing her daughter. "Come in, come in. Don't mind the mess. I was distracting myself with baking instead of cleaning. What can I say?"

Stewart followed Penny inside the small home. They entered straight into a living room with a coat closet opposite the front door. He wiped his shoes on a mat, and Sarah disappeared into the kitchen and came out a moment later with a plate of chocolate chunk cookies made with chocolate batter and white chocolate chunks. He was already sugared out from last night, but he'd have to be polite.

"When things are crazy, I turn to comfort food," Sarah said. "Have a seat."

Penny headed for the couch, and Stewart let her settle in with her mother beside her, and then he took a chair kitty-corner to the women so she could watch Sarah's reactions better.

"I imagine this was all quite a shock," Stewart said.

"You can say that again," Sarah replied. "Ever since my *daet* disappeared, I thought he'd left us."

"Because your mother said so?" he asked.

"Because I saw the argument before he stomped out," she retorted. "He said he was leaving with or without us, and *Mamm* made it clear she was going nowhere."

"When was that?" he asked. "Can you remember the time of day?"

"Not really. I know it was daytime. From talking to my mother over the years, I believe it was late afternoon. But memories can be tricky."

Stewart nodded sympathetically. "What

does it mean to you now that you know he didn't leave you?"

"It means—" Tears welled in Sarah's eyes. "It means my father loved me—loved *us*—after all." She swallowed hard and reached over to squeeze Penny's hand. "It was formative when we believed he'd left. I couldn't believe that my father would walk away from me and never come back. Not care how I was doing, or want to take care of me. It left a father-shaped hole inside of me. I spent the rest of my life trying to fill it with the wrong kind of man. I've finally stopped—just dug in my heels and said no more, you know? And now, I find out that he hadn't stopped loving us, after all, and I've been crying like a baby ever since I found out."

She dabbed at her eyes with a wadded-up tissue.

"We're going to figure out who might have killed him, Mom," Penny said. "So like I told you, we need to figure out who was at the house that day. It might help us figure out who might have had reason to kill your father."

"Yes, and I thought long and hard about it last night," Sarah said, digging in her jeans pocket, and coming out with a piece of paper. "I wrote down everyone I remembered concretely. So it's not a long list. There were more people than this present."

"That's okay," Stewart said. "I appreciate your forthrightness about what you can fully recall. That's helpful."

"My cousins, Tabitha, Hosea and Joel were there," Sarah said. "I was glad to see them, and when *Daet* didn't come home, we sat together on the step, and I felt better knowing they were with me. That means that their parents must have been there— my mother's sister, Miriam, and my uncle Menno. I don't remember seeing them, though, so I don't know if that's useful."

"Mammie mentioned them," Penny murmured.

"How old were your cousins?" Stewart asked.

"Tabitha was my age, and the boys were younger than me."

So not suspects on his list, although they might remember something. She rattled off a few more Amish names of distant relatives she recalled seeing because they'd brought something memorable, or she'd seen her mother tearfully hug them.

"And then there was the police officer," Sarah said. "I don't remember how he was friends with my father, but he was. My father had a way with *Englishers*. He wasn't scared of them, or intimidated by their differences. And that particular police officer had become a family friend."

"What was his name?" Stewart asked.

"We called him Officer Robbie. But I don't recall a last name. I'm sorry."

Stewart jotted it down. A local cop, first name Robert. He couldn't be too hard to track down.

"Did anyone look for your father?" Stewart asked.

"*Yah*, they went around the property, but

with so many people coming and going, someone said they saw *Daet* get into a car." Her Pennsylvania Dutch accent was coming out as she sifted through her memories, Stewart noticed.

"They thought they saw him?" Penny cut in.

"Obviously they were mistaken," Sarah replied. "Because he was dead."

"We don't know that, actually," Stewart said. "It's very likely, but it's possible he wasn't dead yet."

"So someone might have killed him, and then brought his body home, but only so far as to dump him into the well?" Sarah asked, shaking her head.

"If they wanted to frame your mother, yeah," he replied.

Sarah's eyebrows went up, and she nodded. "This is going to be incredibly complicated, isn't it?"

"It might be." He pressed his lips together for a moment. "Do you recall who said they'd seen him get into a car?"

Sarah shook her head. "No, I don't. But that piece of information had confirmed for us what we already believed—that he was gone and he'd left us."

"Do you remember how people reacted to the idea of your father abandoning the family?"

"Shock. Outrage. Anger. Some said he'd smarten up and come home once he cooled off..."

"And your mother?" he asked.

Sarah was silent for a moment. "She went white. I remember thinking she might pass out. Then she sat down and she put a hand over her mouth, and she started to cry. I'd never seen my mother cry like that before. I'd seen her angry, and dash a tear off her cheek, but never like that. I remember thinking that I'd never seen my mother so broken in all my life..."

Sarah sucked in a wavering breath. "I went outside alone after that. My brothers and sisters were in the house with *Mamm*, and I stood out in the drive staring at the road, praying as hard as I could that *Gott* would bring my father home again. I prayed and prayed…" She cleared her throat. "For all the good that did."

"Is that when you stopped believing in the faith?" Penny asked softly.

"Yes. The next morning, when the sun rose and the day began without him and I somehow knew he was gone for good. That was when my faith evaporated. If *Gott* could hear that prayer of a little girl who needed her *daet* and not answer, then he was no God for me."

Penny squeezed her mother's hand again and Sarah straightened.

"Do you remember if Uncle Isaac was there?" Penny asked.

"I think so…" Sarah sighed. "And he's your *mammi*'s last living sibling, so it would be good to talk to him. He might remember more."

"That's what I was thinking…" Penny murmured.

"I'm sorry to bring up all these painful memories," Stewart said quietly.

"Now that I know my father was dead, not just avoiding us, I feel…freer," Sarah said. "But it will take time to process it all, I think."

"I can appreciate that," he replied. "If you remember anything else, tell Penny, okay?"

Sarah nodded. "Of course." She nudged the plate of cookies toward him on the coffee table. "Have some cookies."

Stewart reached for one and took a bite. It was as tasty as it looked, but all he wanted right now was something plain and unsweetened.

"And I'm sorry to hurry you out, but I have to get dressed properly and get into the office. They knew I was arriving late, but I still have the accounts payables to do."

Sarah was a bookkeeper for a local company. He knew that from Penny, and he stood up.

"Thanks for your time," he said.

"I'll see you later, Mom." Penny leaned over and gave her mother a hug.

"Certainly," Sarah said as she released Penny. "And feel free to come by again, Stewart. You're always welcome here."

He smiled back. Hopefully he still would be at the end of this investigation.

FOUR

As the door shut behind them, Penny felt like a vise around her chest released. It wasn't that her mother caused her stress, exactly, but this preoccupation with *Dawdie*'s abandonment of the family had a weight of its own...even now that they knew he had died, and not actually left. Now, as a family, they would have to adjust to this new reality. There would be anger, Penny thought, after the sorrow, especially once Sarah got around to realizing how much emotional damage she'd endured, how much fallout there had been for an abandonment that had never happened.

How would their lives have been different if they'd known he was dead, grieved it and been able to move on? There would have been trauma, but would there have been less trauma in the lives of his surviving children? If they'd known their father loved them and that he had never chosen to leave them early, would it have changed the choices they made, and the relationships that attracted them? That was a loaded question, though, because if Sarah had picked a different husband, Penny never would have been born.

Stewart led the way to their parked cruiser, half a step ahead of her, and she was glad he was here. Stewart normalized things somehow…just having his stable presence meant that all of this shifting sand didn't swallow her.

"Should we head out to Little Dusseldorf, then?" Penny asked.

"I think so," he replied. "Your grandmother's place first?"

"Let's stop at Uncle Isaac's," she replied. "It's a little more out of the way, and I want to try and talk to him before my grandfather's death is common knowledge. Then we can spend a bit more time with my grandmother."

"I think that's a good idea. Where does he live?" Stewart asked.

"He's living with my cousin—Isaac's son, Jacob."

"Seriously?" For a non-church attender, Stewart never missed a beat when it came to Biblical connections.

"The Amish enjoy Biblical patterns in names." She cast him a wry smile. "I'm completely serious. Isaac's dad's name was Abe. So they had Abraham, Isaac and Jacob. Jacob let the pattern go, though, when he had five daughters. They live about fifteen miles from my grandmother's place."

"Let's see if we can get an adult perspective—as in someone who was an adult at the time Caleb was killed," Stewart said. "How are his faculties?"

"Sharp, last I saw him about a year ago," she replied.

Penny got into the driver's seat of the

cruiser once more. She slammed the door and put on her seat belt. Stewart did the same. For a moment, she just sat there, and she looked past Stewart toward the town-house. She could only imagine the turmoil of emotions her mother was going through right now.

"You okay?" Stewart asked quietly.

"Yeah…"

"Is your mom okay?" he asked. "You'd know better than anyone."

That was true, and her mother was obviously shaken up, but Sarah was a pro at simply moving forward. She'd been through a lot in her life, and Penny had watched her mother gather up her courage and take the next step time after time. Breakup after breakup.

"It's called generational trauma," Penny said, putting the car into gear and pulling out into traffic. "I learned about it in college. You see it in a lot of families. For example, people who lived through the Great Depression were more likely to hoard goods. They were afraid of something big happening again that would affect their ability to provide for their families, and they'd keep absolutely everything after that. Buttons, pieces of string, wires, bottles… And that learned behavior was passed down to the next generation. They'd be holding on to buttons and string because Mom always did, and it just felt wrong to throw them away, even though that generation had never experienced the Great Depression."

Traffic was light that morning, but other drivers still gave them a respectfully wide berth in their cruiser. Penny stopped at a red light, and she looked over to see a wide-eyed youngster in the back seat of a car staring at her. She smiled and the kid smiled back.

"You can also see it in families that had an alcoholic parent," Penny went on. The light turned green and she stepped on the gas. "There will be coping mechanisms that the children learn, and they'll use those coping strategies in later relationships, and unconsciously teach them to their children, too. You'll see the grandchildren of alcoholics using coping strategies typically seen in relationships that include a substance abuser, and neither partner even drinks. It's a learned pattern."

Penny liked to understand things. She liked to line them up and make sense of them. Nothing irritated her more than something that didn't make sense...and Caleb's death made no sense. She glanced over at Stewart, and he was watching her with a thoughtful look on his face.

"What?" she said.

"What generational trauma are you carrying around?" he asked.

"All sorts, I'm sure," she replied with a wry smile. "I've seen patterns in my own family—not patterns with alcoholism, but with relationships. We all are less inclined to trust. We don't see weddings and assume the couple will stay united for the rest of their lives. We're...jaded."

"The second generation after your grand-father disappeared," he said.

"Well...my dad left, too," she reminded him. "So if I'm jaded, I have some good reasons."

Stewart smiled faintly. "Not every guy will leave you, Pen."

"I know. Theoretically," she replied, shooting him a teasing smile. "Look at you—three years of being my partner, and you still show up for work every day."

"I'm serious," he said. "There are men who want a lifelong relationship with one person as much as you do."

He was tough to avoid when he got ear-nest, but Penny didn't need Stewart's reas-surances that good guys existed. She knew they did. Stewart was one of them, but she wasn't the type of woman who necessarily ended up with a guy like Stewart. Stewart liked boundaries and balance, and Penny threw all of her mixed-up feelings into the pressure cooker of her job, and kept them at bay that way. Every woman thought she'd found a good guy when she got married. *Mammi* had thought so, and maybe she had after all. But Penny's mother had thought so, too, and she'd been wrong. Twice. Penny had seen other friends get married with just as much optimism and love, only to be divorced ten years later. And Penny didn't think her heart could survive a mangling like that. Truth be told, she was scared, and it took a lot of genuine optimism to take a leap like marriage. Penny's optimism in relationships had been more determined, and a little less genuine.

"I should point out that you're just as single as I am," she said.

"I know. My mother is trying desperately to set me up with available women in her church," he replied.

"So why haven't you settled own with one of those nice women?" Penny asked.

"I don't know," he replied with a shrug. "Maybe I'm complicated."

Penny snorted out a laugh.

"I'm not complicated?" he chuckled.

"Not very," she replied.

"So why am I single, then?" he challenged her.

"I doubt you will be for terribly long," she said. "You just haven't met her yet. You're a catch, Stew. You'll find some woman you adore, and you'll take the leap. It's in your nature."

"I'm the marrying kind, am I?" he laughed.

"Aren't you?"

"Yeah, I guess I am."

She pulled onto the highway and headed toward the part of the county where many Amish lived. She settled back into her seat as she pulled into the right-hand lane for a comfortable drive.

"You never talk about your dad," Stewart said.

"There's not much to say," she said.

"How often do you see him?" he asked.

"From time to time. He took me out for dinner the weekend after my birthday last year."

"I remember that," he said. "That's the last time you saw him?"

"In person, yes," she replied. "But we keep up. We chat sometimes." She was silent for a moment, remembering when she last talked with her father on the phone. He was remarried now, and she had two stepsiblings who were both in high school. "It's not my father being in my life that was ever a problem. He's been in my life. He loves me. I know that. It's my dad not being in my mother's life—that's the thing that stung for me. He'll always love me because I'm his daughter. But he stopped loving my mother—there was an expiration date on their love. And that…affected me."

"Yeah," Stewart said softly.

"You get it?" Penny asked, and she glanced over at him.

Stewart always seemed pure as the driven snow with his happy, functional family of origin. But her parents' split had wounded her deeply. She was a lot like her mother in personality and looks. They were both no-nonsense types, and they liked to get things done. And Penny did want a love that would last. While she was glad she had her father in her life, the kind of relationship she wanted was romantic, and she needed to be able to trust a man to stand by her through thick and thin as her partner in life. A dad would love his daughter no matter what. But a husband—could a husband even last in her family line?

"Yeah, I get it," Stewart said.

And they fell into companionable silence. Sometimes it was easier not to talk about things, but to be understood was still a comfort.

As they got closer to the Amish farming area, the roads narrowed, the speed limits lowered, and Amish buggies became a more common sight. Horses clopped along, some at a slower pace than others, carrying Amish families about their business. The Amish areas just slowed down, like stepping back in time. Stewart had always liked that about these parts of Pennsylvania—as if the very air they breathed here was different.

He was passionate about his job as detective, finding answers and providing justice. In order for everyone to enjoy a safe society, bad guys needed to be caught and punished. But there always would be a part of him that yearned for some quiet and peace. He needed something to balance out the ugliness he saw at work, to remind him that life was beautiful and people were still good. Amish country provided that...most times.

Amish country provided that for a lot of people. That was why they came out to the Amish markets and shopped for Amish-made quilts, furniture, baskets... The workmanship was always top-notch, but it was more than that. It was a connection to a community that felt more unsullied than it really was, and Stewart wasn't the only one who needed it.

Penny knew her way around these rural

roads and highways, and Stewart had no concern that she wouldn't get them where they needed to go. She slowed and made a turn onto a narrow gravel road, then sped up again. He could see dust billowing out behind them in the side mirror. Ever since that pickup truck, they'd both been watching those mirrors a little more closely.

They crested a knoll, and beneath them Amish farms spread out across the hills and dales. Small herds of cattle in lush pasture, crop fields in various hues of yellow and green, red barns, white houses, and one field filled with sheep—if Stewart's guess was right—but it was hard to tell from this distance.

"That's Jacob's farm right at the bottom of the hill," Penny said. "It's a beautiful property."

It was. One day, when he retired from policing, Stewart wanted to buy his own little plot of land and get himself a few chickens. He'd plant a massive garden and spend his days tending it. He'd have a couple of outdoor cats, a big lazy dog, and he'd put his feet up on his porch at the end of a day and watch the sunset. That was his idea of a well-deserved rest.

But they weren't here to get pulled into the beauty, and Stewart wasn't retired yet.

"I think we should ask our questions in relation to your missing grandfather, not your dead grandfather," Stewart said. "And see what they say."

"I suppose it's best to tell *Mammi* before we tell her local family," Penny agreed. Her mother had promised not to reveal the identity of the body until Penny had a chance to talk to her.

But it was more than that. Stewart wanted to see if old Great-Uncle Isaac was going to lie.

They pulled into the drive that led up to a white farmhouse. Beyond was a large chicken coop, and past that, a barn. An old man sat on the front porch, a knife and piece of wood in his hands as he whittled away at something. He watched the cruiser park, then rose to his feet and came down the steps.

Penny got out of the cruiser first, calling out as she walked.

"Hello, Uncle!" she said. "It's Penny—Sarah's daughter, Elizabeth's granddaughter."

Stewart got out of the vehicle and did a 360, looking over the property in a quick scan. The side door opened and a middle-aged Amish woman poked her head out the screen door.

"Is that you, Penny?"

"Aunt May!"

Stewart waited as they said their hellos. It was interesting to see Penny with any family, let alone the Amish side of her family. He'd heard enough of their stories over the years. How well did he really know her, though? Yesterday, he would have said he knew her better than anyone, but today, he wasn't so sure.

"This is my partner, Stewart," she said, and Stewart stepped up next to her.

"We don't want to take up too much of your time," Stewart said, "but we're investigating a missing person—Caleb Renno."

"Caleb? Aunt Elizabeth's husband?" May said. "Your grandfather, I should say, Penny."

"Yes, we are looking into his disappearance," Penny replied.

"I never knew him," May said. "I'm too young, but my father-in-law knew him, of course."

"That's why we stopped by," Penny replied. "I wanted to ask Great-Uncle Isaac what he remembered from that night he disappeared."

"Come inside, and I'll get you something to eat," May said.

"*Yah, yah,*" the old man said. "I was there the night he left."

"It's terrible to think of all that poor Elizabeth went through," May said, and she paused on the step and shaded her eyes. "I don't see my husband."

"It's okay," Penny said. "I'd love to see Jacob again, but today, we really needed to talk to Uncle Isaac."

They all went inside together, Stewart taking up the rear. The kitchen looked like most Amish kitchens—clean and tidy, and with a similar layout. There was a big black stove dominating one wall, a heavy wooden table where the family would eat their meals and a plenty of counter space. The floors weren't hardwood—they were polished sheets of particle board, the color deep and golden from linseed oil. It made the room look larger somehow, but it was cozy and comfortable all the same.

May brought a plate of oatmeal cookies to the table, then went to the icebox and pulled out a pitcher of meadow tea. It took a few moments for everyone to get settled around the table. May didn't sit down. Instead she puttered around the kitchen, but she kept an eye on the conversation.

"So, Uncle Isaac," Penny said, leaning forward. "We wanted to ask you about that night when my grandfather disappeared. Do you remember it?"

"Of course I remember it," he replied. "Everything changed for my older sister. Everything."

Stewart pulled out a notepad and clicked his pen open. "When did you arrive that evening?"

"Oh… Well, now…" Isaac stroked his white beard. "I arrived with my sister Miriam and her husband Menno. I remember that Miriam was very upset about Elizabeth and Caleb's financial situation. That stands out in my memory. Everyone was banding together to makes sure they had enough food."

"How did Caleb respond to that?" he asked.

"He was already in a foul mood when we arrived. He thanked us grudgingly for our gifts of food, and then he pulled Elizabeth aside and was talking rather harshly to her."

There was a murmur from May, and Isaac's gaze flickered in her direction.

"It's okay," Penny said. "*Mammi* already told us they had a big fight."

"That they did," Isaac said. "Or at least, I saw the end of it. He was furious that she'd told us about their difficulties. He'd said she didn't trust him. And I don't know why I got the feeling, but it seemed like Caleb was jealous about some other man. Although that was ridiculous because Elizabeth was a good and proper woman. So that made me mad—I remember that. I was really angry on my sister's behalf. Caleb said he could get work no problem in another community, and if she was choosing us over him, then he'd go make the money on his own."

"So he was he leaving her?" Penny asked.

"Well…it's hard to tell now, isn't it?" Isaac replied. "I didn't think that was what was happening. I was just a young man then and I didn't know about married relationships, so I remember being pretty startled by it all. I was upset that he'd raised his voice to my sister, and that he'd suggest she'd be anything but faithful to him. He went stomping out, and Elizabeth tried to pretend that everything was fine, and then she started crying, and Miriam was trying to comfort her, and Menno and I just looked at each other. I honestly didn't think I'd seen a man just abandon his family."

"Did you see him again that night?" Stewart asked.

Isaac's brow furrowed for a moment, then he shook his head. "Not that I remember. I don't think I did. I do remember a few hours later I went outside and looked around trying to find Caleb because Elizabeth was upset and the *kinner* were upset, too. I had it in my head that I'd calm him down and bring him back inside. But I couldn't find him. Someone said they saw him get into a car."

"Who said that?" Stewart asked.

"I don't remember… Maybe one of my cousins? I don't recall. But someone said he'd left in a car, and I remember that because *Englisher* automobiles were a big taboo, of course. Back then, we had a bishop who was even stricter than the bishop now. And we used to need special permission to even hire a van."

"So, he left in the car…" Penny prompted.

"*Yah*, and we stayed very late, waiting for him to come home before we left so we could tell him we were sorry for upsetting him. We didn't want to leave Elizabeth alone like that. But then she finally insisted that we leave, and we were all very tired, so we did."

"And then?" Penny asked softly.

Isaac spread his hands. "Over the next few days, Elizabeth got more and more frantic. She kept saying that he'd cool off and come home, and then when he didn't, I overheard her telling our mother that she thought he'd left her."

"Did anyone search for him?" Stewart asked. "I mean, if someone just vanishes, there's always the chance of accident or something, isn't there?"

"*Yah*, we did. We looked along roads, and called hospitals, and we looked through the trees, too."

"No one thought to look in the well?" Penny asked.

That was tipping their hand just a bit, but she was right to ask it. Why not look in the well?

"The well?" Isaac's eyes widened. "The body found in Elizabeth's well! You think it's him?"

Penny made a noncommittal noise.

"I don't know what to tell you," Isaac said. "We did our best. Because of the story of him leaving in a car, we focused more on roads, and we even put up some missing-person signs in town. And as for the well, it was sealed up, I recall. It didn't occur to us."

"Did anyone mention seeing him?" Stewart asked. Because if the man was dead and someone mentioned him, they might be trying to create a false trail.

Isaac shook his head. "No one. He was just...gone. And Elizabeth kept saying he'd come back. For years, she said he'd come back to see the *kinner*, at least, and then she'd give him a piece of her mind about all he'd put them through. But he never did." The old man's gaze flickered between them. "The body in the well—is it his?"

"We can't say," Stewart said. "We're pursuing a few different leads here."

Isaac cast Penny an apologetic look. "Your *mamm* and her brothers and sisters were so upset. And we just did our best to help out and keep food on their table. Elizabeth couldn't even remarry because her husband was still living."

"Her only hope was him returning," Penny murmured.

"I'm afraid so."

For a moment, everyone was silent. Isaac dropped his gaze and May shuffled her feet.

"I wanted to ask a few more things about Caleb," Stewart said. "When he was living with his family, did anyone ever see him around people who might be considered... dangerous?"

Isaac shrugged. "I mean, he did have an inordinate amount of *Englisher* friends."

There was silence again, and May cleared her throat.

"No offense intended, of course," May said. "But Amish folk tend to be closest to other Amish folk. We sell to *Englishers*, and sometimes we get to know them, but they'll never really understand us, will they? So having an *Englisher* friend is... okay. It's normal. But having a few?" May spread her hands. "That's why everyone thinks Caleb went *English*."

"No offense, of course," Isaac added, giving him a pained look.

"It's okay," Stewart said. He glanced over at Penny. This was where she'd need to take over.

"Really, it's fine," Penny said, taking his

cue. "You know that I understand all this. So…how many *Englishers* did he spend time with?"

"He chatted with a lot of them in town," Isaac said. "The shop owners, the regulars. They all knew him in Little Dusseldorf. And he had *Englishers* who'd come to see him sometimes—people we didn't know—and Elizabeth used to worry about it. She said it would look bad."

"Did she mention who they were?" Penny pressed.

"I don't know. You should ask her about that," Isaac said. "But he was an Amish man with a lot more *Englisher* connections than really made sense. It was like he was drawn to them, somehow. Or they were drawn to him. Maybe we should have seen the writing on the wall with him."

"In what way?" Stewart asked.

"In that he abandoned his wife and five *kinner* and went *English*," Isaac said.

Stewart exchanged a look with Penny. It was a strange detail to matter so much to these people, but it obviously did matter. Too many outsider connections. What did that mean? It might mean that the one who killed Caleb hadn't been Amish. Or, it might mean that Isaac knew more than he was letting on, and was trying to shift the blame outside their community.

Old men could seem harmless enough at their advanced age, but it didn't mean they'd always been so. Stewart made a couple of notes in his notebook and snapped it shut.

"Do you have any guesses as to who the dead man in the well was?" Stewart asked.

May just shrugged, but Isaac looked thoughtful for a moment. "A traveler, maybe?"

"And how would he have gotten into Elizabeth's well?" Stewart asked.

"I don't know that… But Elizabeth would not be involved. That's for sure and certain. She's a good, devout woman."

These were all good, devout people. That

was the problem. But someone had killed Caleb.

"Thank you, Uncle," Penny said. "We appreciate it. We'll talk with *Mammi* again and see if she can give us more clarity about those *Englisher* friends."

Stewart watched the old man's face for signs of distress over them double-checking his story, but either Isaac hid his feelings well, or there was nothing to hide.

"We'd better get going," Stewart said, and he touched Penny's elbow.

"Yes," she said, and she stood up. "We'll let you all know what we find out when the investigation is over."

May nodded, but her expression stayed somber. Whatever they unearthed, Stewart had a feeling it was going to make a difference for a lot of people. The Amish were connected, and whoever had killed Caleb probably had grandchildren by now—a whole family line to bear the shame. And if the murderer was Amish, this community had a lot to deal with.

FIVE

"Can you drive?" Penny asked, tossing the keys toward Stewart. He caught them in the air. "I want to make a few notes while things are fresh."

"Sure." He cast her an easy smile, and like always, her stomach hovered just a bit when he grinned at her like that. But that was Stew for you—far too charming for his own good.

Penny got into the passenger side, buckled up and then pulled out her phone. She wanted to keep track of who had heard the story about Caleb leaving in a car, and see if she could narrow down who had actually seen him leave...if he *had* left. Because if he'd left with someone, that person just might be his killer, or might have seen who he was last with before he died. And if he hadn't left…whoever started that rumor had a reason to want everyone to believe he'd driven off…

Stewart started the car, and Penny looked out the window to see if anyone had come outside to see them off. Isaac and May had stayed inside, and Jacob was still nowhere to be seen, probably working on his farm somewhere.

"So, what do you think?" Stewart asked.

"First of all, it's weird that Caleb had so many *Englisher* friends," she said.

"No offense intended," Stewart said with a low laugh.

"Of course." She chuckled. "It's just the way they are. You don't keep a uniquely different community without some solid boundaries. Otherwise, change would creep in. People's friendships influence them, and the Amish are nothing if not dedicated to keeping things exactly the same."

"I know, I know," he said. "So…you

think it's strange, too, he'd have so many outside influences."

"Very strange. Downright weird," she replied.

"Are you ready to tell your grandmother the identity of the body?" he asked.

"Yeah, I think we'd better," she replied, and to her surprise, her voice was strong. Because she didn't feel as capable as she sounded right now. This was big news— life-altering news... And *Mammi* needed to know now, before word got to her from other sources.

Penny pulled her mind back to the case, and made a few more notes in her phone while Stewart drove them to *Mammi*'s place. It wasn't far, and when they arrived, Penny spotted her grandmother in the garden. She was on her hands and knees, pulling weeds into an ice cream bucket.

Elizabeth looked up, shaded her eyes and then slowly began to push herself to her feet. By the time Penny got out of the car, *Mammi* was standing and brushing off the front of her dress, which was soiled from the dirt.

"Hello?" her grandmother called out, sounding a little confused to Penny's ear.

"Hi, *Mammi*," Penny said, crossing the lawn.

"Who are you?" *Mammi* asked, frowning. "Do you know where Willard is?"

"*Mammi*, it's Penny. I'm your granddaughter. I'm Sarah's daughter."

"Sarah's daughter?" the older woman frowned, but Penny could see some recognition coming back into those watery blue eyes.

"Yes, *Mammi*. I'm Penny."

"Where's Willard?"

Penny shook her head. "Who's Willard?"

"My husband. Willard went out. Where is he now?"

Her husband? Penny glanced over her shoulder to see that Stewart was a few feet behind her. His eyebrows went up, too.

"You mean Caleb," Penny said gently. "Your husband's name was Caleb, *Mammi*."

"Willard goes out sometimes, and he doesn't tell me before he leaves how long he'll be. And that isn't nice, you know." Her grandmother's lips quivered. "It's only considerate to tell your wife how long you'll be so she doesn't worry. And he left without telling me that."

Willard. What was this preoccupation with a man named Willard?

"You mean Caleb," Penny repeated.

Mammi blinked a couple of times. "What did I say?"

"You said Willard. Who is that?"

"I meant Caleb," she replied, and she brushed some dirt off her hands.

"*Mammi,* do you know who I am?" Penny asked gently.

Her grandmother blinked at her, then smiled faintly. "Of course I do. Don't be silly."

"It's Penny."

"I know that, Penny."

Okay, so she was back in the present now. That was good.

"I'm sorry, dear. I get a little turned around sometimes."

"It's okay, *Mammi*," Penny said gently. "Do you want to come inside? We wanted to talk to you about something."

"What about?" *Mammi* asked, but she allowed Penny to steer her toward the house.

Stewart opened the door for them and stood back as Penny guided her grandmother inside. *Mammi* seemed more herself now, and she went to the kitchen sink and washed the dark soil off her hands.

"You were worried about your husband being late," Stewart said quietly.

"I do that sometimes," *Mammi* said. "I get a little lost in the past... You wait until you're my age, and then you won't judge me for it."

"We aren't judging you, *Mammi*," Penny said. "It's okay. It was a hard time, wasn't it?"

"It was a horrible time," her grandmother replied. "For several months after he left me, I was certain he'd come back with some very good reason for having been away."

"What kind of reason?" Stewart asked.

She shook her head and dried her hands on a tea towel. "I would know it when I heard it, wouldn't I?"

Penny gestured to the kitchen table. "Why don't you sit down? We want to tell you what we discovered about the body in the well."

"Oh." Her grandmother nodded and then went over to a chair. After she was seated, she looked up at them expectantly. "Who is it?"

"We checked the dental records against Caleb's," Penny said. "And the body in the well…is his."

Mammi frowned again, then shook her head. "No, that can't be."

"I'm afraid it's conclusive, ma'am," Stewart said. "That body belongs to your husband, Caleb Renno. He didn't leave you after all. He was killed."

"Someone killed my Caleb?" *Mammi*

kept shaking her head. "But who would do that? Maybe it was an accident! Maybe he fell into the well?"

"No, ma'am." Stewart's voice was quiet but firm. Penny knew the drill here—facts were important, and people didn't need false hope or comforting explanations. They needed the facts. "The position of the body in the well compared to the wound on the skull meant that it wasn't an accident. Your husband was murdered."

Color drained from *Mammi*'s face and she sat in stunned silence. Penny reached out and took her grandmother's limp hand.

"*Mammi*, it means that Caleb didn't abandon you," Penny said softly. "He didn't leave you. He didn't stop loving you! Someone killed him—that's why he didn't come back. Not because he was leaving you and the kids."

Her grandmother slowly looked over at Penny, tears welling in her eyes. "He didn't leave me…"

"No, *Mammi*. Caleb didn't leave you."

The first tear trickled down her cheek, and she exhaled a shuddering breath.

"He didn't walk out on me and the *kinner*?" She didn't seem to be talking to Penny anymore, though. "He didn't leave us… He didn't get angry at me and…and stop loving me…"

Mammi covered her face with her soft, wrinkled hands and her shoulders began to shake. Her sobs were silent at first, and then she couldn't seem to hold in the pressure of her emotions as she wept into her hands.

Penny stood up and went around the table, wrapping her arms around her grandmother's shaking shoulders. Mammi leaned into the embrace and Penny felt her own tears standing in her eyes in response. She'd never known this grandfather, and truthfully, she'd never liked him. He'd been the cause of so much heartbreak in her own family, but seeing how the news of his death forty-eight years in the past had cut her grandmother to the core showed her how much he'd meant to the family. Somehow, Penny was going to have to change her view of Caleb, too, but a lifetime of resentment was hard to let go of all at once.

It took a couple of minutes for *Mammi*'s sobs to subside, and she straightened out of Penny's arms again. Stewart seemed to have come up with some tissues because he handed them to her. *Mammi* blew her nose and wiped her eyes again.

"I thought he was alive still..." *Mammi* looked up at Penny. "I thought he was out there with his electricity and roaring cars, and that he was still alive. I thought maybe one day his conscience would get the better of him and he'd come back to see what became of us. I imagined his whole life—replacing me and the *kinner* with a whole other family..." She dabbed at her eyes again. "But he was *dead*."

"Yes, he was dead," Penny said.

"I have to forgive him for not coming home, then," she said, shaking her head. "It wasn't his fault. He had a terribly good reason, after all, didn't he? It was the excuse that I couldn't deny…"

"Elizabeth, I need to ask you about Willard," Stewart said, as he pulled the chair out and sat down facing the old woman.

"Oh…" *Mammi*'s voice quavered.

"Who is Willard?" he asked.

"That's Caleb," she said softly. "You see…" Her gaze flickered toward Penny apologetically. "That's the biggest reason I thought he'd gone *English*. He was born *English*. He converted to the Amish faith a few years before I met him, and when he converted he changed his name to something more Amish so he could blend in."

"Changed his name?" Penny murmured.

"He wanted an Amish life. A real one, not always being Willard—the one whose name stood out."

"Being Amish is more than a name," Penny said. "What about the language?"

"Oh, he spoke Pennsylvania Dutch fluently by the time I met him," *Mammi* said. "He was very good with languages.

He spoke English, of course, and German. Knowing German made picking up Pennsylvania Dutch much easier, since it's a German dialect. And somehow, he was able to get the accent, too. He was just… very skilled in languages."

"No one suspected?" Stewart asked.

"Well, my generation knew, but we didn't tell the *kinner.*" *Mammi* spread her hands. "Some things are for adults to know and others are for the younger ones. He was baptized into the church, was an Amish man in good standing, and if you didn't know he'd converted, you wouldn't guess. No one else did, as a matter of fact."

Penny's heart thudded hard in her throat. Her grandfather had been born *English* and had slid seamlessly into an Amish community complete with language and culture, and had simply taken up a whole new life. Who did that?

"And he told you about it?" Penny asked.

"Of course. We Amish don't take marriage lightly. He said I needed to know everything before I married him."

"What was his name before?" Stewart's gaze locked on Elizabeth's face.

"Willard Morrison."

"Why did he change his name?" Stewart asked.

"To blend in better with our community."

"That's it? Just to…blend in?"

"*Yah.*"

"Did he do it for you, maybe?" Penny asked.

"No, he'd changed it already. And to his credit, he could have just kept his mouth shut and I'd never have been the wiser. He could have said he was from Indiana or something."

"Are you sure he didn't have a history in the military or something? Was he a spy, perhaps?" Penny asked.

"No."

"Was he afraid of something?" Stewart pressed.

"Not that he ever mentioned to me,"

Mammi replied. "But he had *Englisher* friends. Many *Englisher* friends. And I didn't like that. It made people talk too much, and if he wanted to blend in, that was not the way to do it."

"Any *Englisher* friends he saw more often than others?" Stewart asked.

"*Yah*. His very best friend was Mike Miller. He owned the old hotel in Little Dusseldorf."

"What was it called?" Penny asked.

"Oh… Slumber Inn, I believe. The one right downtown on Main. The only one on Main Street."

"We heard about a police officer— Officer Robbie?" Penny said.

"He was another one of my husband's friends. He was respectful of our community and we all really liked him."

"What became of him?" Stewart asked.

She just shook her head. "When my husband vanished, Officer Robbie stopped coming by. It wouldn't have been appropriate anyway."

Stewart made a note in his notebook and closed it.

"*Mammi*, can we drop you off at Jacob's place, perhaps? We have to get going, but I don't want to just leave you alone."

"I would prefer to be left alone, dear," *Mammi* said. "I know you think I can't handle myself, but I can. And I need some time alone to process all of this and do some praying. I'm not ready for my brother Isaac or anyone else right now. I need to pray."

And Penny could understand that sentiment rather well. She was the same in the face of a big shock—she just wanted time alone with God to get her balance again.

"Okay," Penny said.

"Besides, I have Linda next door. She'll check on me. She always does."

Mammi had family and her Amish community, which was a far sight more than a lot of people had these days. And she had God, too.

Penny gave her grandmother another

hug. "There are some police officers still working out there with the well. If you need me, you just go find one of them and they'll radio me, okay?"

"Of course, dear." *Mammi* rose to her feet. "You go find who killed my husband. That will help me more than anything—to know why he died like that."

And that was all that Penny could offer. This was one cold case that Penny needed to see resolved. Caleb might be dead, but he left some very real hearts behind. And they needed closure.

Stewart led the way to the car, and he kept the keys. Whatever Penny said right now, she needed to process, not drive. They stopped by the excavation site, where they were still sifting through the bottom sediment in the well, and he made sure that the troopers there would check in on old Mrs. Renno a few times throughout the afternoon and radio them if she needed anything. His mind was clicking forward to the things that needed doing—Elizabeth's needs, the case, but above everything else, he was thinking about Penny.

Penny slid wordlessly into the passenger seat, and as Stewart got back into the car, he looked over at her. She looked pale now, withdrawn.

"Are you okay?" he asked.

"I didn't think it would hit me this hard," she said. "I didn't know him, Stew. He's just…a story. I never met him. I never heard a good thing about him…"

"But he's still your grandfather," he replied quietly. He reached over and caught her hand.

"Yeah, I'm starting to feel that," she said. Her fingers closed over his in a tight squeeze.

"You sure you don't want to hand this off to someone else?" he asked. "You've done your duty by your grandmother, and you could tap out now, if you wanted to."

She shook her head. "Duty isn't done until I figure out who did it, Stew."

He knew what she meant, and he couldn't talk her out of it. He'd just wanted to offer her a way out of this investigation, in case she needed it.

"I think we have the best chance of solving the case, honestly," Penny went on.

And they probably did, with Penny's family connections and her insights into the Amish world. But while her highest concern was the killer, his was his partner. The killer had been running loose for almost fifty years, and Penny had just received a big shock. He gave her hand another squeeze, and she returned it, giving him a wan smile.

"You want to talk it out?" he asked.

"Yes, please."

A smile tugged at her lips, and just the way she said it made his heartbeat skip. Penny was tough as nails, but underneath that armor was a lot of warmth and softness that most people didn't get the chance to see.

Stewart released her hand and put the

car into gear. Would she want to talk about how all of this made her feel? About what it did to her family as a whole? About what it meant to her now that her grandfather wasn't the bad guy who'd abandoned his family?

"Okay, where do you want to start?" he asked.

"He changed his name," Penny said. "That's weird, right? He changed his name from—" she checked her phone "—Willard Morrison to Caleb Renno. Why do that? And he got married, had kids. He told his wife about the name change…and he kept all sorts of *Englisher* friends. Who does that?"

"Right. So you want to talk about the case," he said.

"Of course! What else are we trying to untangle here?"

"Your feelings, maybe?" Stewart said, shaking his head. Penny was like that— she'd evade her own emotions and prioritize whatever case they were working on.

"My feelings can wait until we've figured out who killed my grandfather," she retorted.

"Can they?" he asked. "Because last I checked, that's not how feelings worked!"

"That's how *my* feelings work," she retorted. "Is this complicated? Yes! But there is no point in focusing on how I feel about a knot when I can just untie it."

"And you can do that?" he asked incredulously. "Ignore your feelings and focus on the knot?"

"Yes. For now. When I'm alone, I'll pray about it and get my balance back."

But not with him. Stewart heaved a sigh. The silly thing was, she was completely capable of cordoning off her feelings in the name of work. She did it constantly. No one worked more overtime hours than his partner did. Stewart looked for balance before he was alone with his feelings. Penny just looked for more work to bury herself in.

"So humor me, Pen," he said. "How are you feeling right now? Just having given your grandmother that kind of news and finding out that your grandfather had some hidden history. How are you feeling?"

"I don't even know," she replied. "I'm all tangled up about it. At least he never left my grandmother high and dry, but who was he? What kind of man gets himself bashed in the head and dumped down a well? What kind of man changes his name and disappears into an Amish community after being raised *English*?"

"What kind?" Stewart asked quietly.

"A bad one. Someone on the run. That's my fear."

Honestly, that was his fear, too.

"If it turns out that my grandfather was a criminal running from justice, it's going to hurt her in a different way," she went on. "It'll hurt my mom, too, and my aunts and uncles."

"And what about you?" he asked.

Penny let out a slow breath. "No, it won't hurt me."

"You sure about that?" Because he

wished she'd open up to him—tell him what was really stewing inside of her.

"I've heard all my life that he was a bad man," Penny said. "It wouldn't change anything, would it? We'd just know more about how bad he was. That's it. The damage is already done there."

Stew nodded. "I guess I understand that."

"But I had a moment of hope there," she said. "When I knew it was my grandfather's body, and I thought that he might have been a good guy who ran into a bad guy…you know? There was a bit of hope that maybe my family history was a little purer and happier than we'd thought. Then we learned about Willard. I'm not speaking for everyone, but me? I need answers."

And there was something inside of Stewart that reared up at those words. Penny needed answers, and he was going to get them. Well, *they* were going to get those answers. Much as he'd like to be her hero right now, their best chance of unravelling this knot was with Penny's insights included. But he wasn't leaving her alone in this. Together, they'd figure out who killed him, and why. And hopefully, once they had a good idea who did it, they could prove it. That was always the catch, wasn't it?

"We'll figure it out," Stewart said. "I'm thinking we should talk with a few more of your family members—the older folks—who would remember Caleb, and see what they can tell us. Then we stop by the Slumber Inn."

"I agree," she said. "Maybe we can get a bigger picture of who my grandfather was. That will help. We need to look into who Willard Morrison really was—his family, friends. I'm also curious about Officer Robbie. He might have some current police connections. You never know."

Stewart agreed and put in a call to the office to start searching records for a Willard Morrison and his name change before they hit the road again.

The first place they stopped was at Elizabeth's sister Miriam's home. She was widowed now, and she remembered Caleb well. Hearing that he had died and hadn't abandoned his family after all did soften her, and she told stories about Caleb that showed a caring, loving family man. She talked about how he'd brought Elizabeth a chicken on their first wedding anniversary, and every anniversary after that. It was a practical way to grow a flock, but it was also a sweet gesture.

She told about how happy he'd been at the birth of each of his children, and how when his first child was born, he'd sat up all night holding his baby boy in his arms so that Elizabeth could sleep. Miriam had been there to help support her sister.

"I was so shocked he'd leave her…that was the thing. He loved his family so much that when I heard he'd just gotten in a car and driven off, I thought maybe his *Englisher* past was calling to him. What else could explain it?"

Besides a murder, of course, Stewart

thought, but it was understandable if people didn't jump to that conclusion.

"Did you see him drive off?" Stewart asked.

Miriam shook her head. "No, someone told me he did."

"Who?"

"My brother, maybe? It's been many years. I hardly remember. We went over that night in our heads again and again after Caleb didn't return, so I suppose we remember better than we might have, but still. Someone said they'd heard he drove off… It was that kind of thing. But I remember specifically that we thought he'd left in a car. I connected it to his *Englisher* friends, of course. There was no reason to believe otherwise. We couldn't find him, and why would our friends and family lie about something like that?"

When they got into the car again after that visit, Stewart looked over at Penny and waited for her to speak. She put on her seat belt, and for a moment, her jaw tensed. He didn't move.

"He loved them," she said at last.

"It sounds like he did."

"I heard about the fights," she said quietly. "I heard about the harsh words. I'd assumed my grandmother was a wonderful person and he was a verbally abusive man."

"Maybe not a full picture of who he was…what they were as a family. It stands to reason that people would remember him differently if they believed he left them. They'd focus on the hard times, and maybe not remember him fairly."

"True… It would be simpler if he'd been a cad, though."

"Simpler to find his killer?" he asked.

"Simpler to hate him." She lifted her gaze to meet his. He could see the emotion swimming in her eyes.

"You don't want to find any redeeming qualities in your grandfather?" he asked.

"If I do, I have to rethink a lot of things, don't I?" she said. "I have to rethink all sorts of things I assumed to be true, or conclusions I jumped to. About him, about my family, about my own life choices."

"It might be worth it," he said. "Penny, I know you pretty well by now, and I've noticed something about you."

Her gaze turned wary.

"You try not to feel things," he went on. "You throw yourself into our cases like they'll distract you from feeling anything."

"That's what you think?" she asked quietly.

"Yeah." He was just being honest. "You work overtime. You bring files home. You stay in the office late, and pore over photos and documents..."

"I'm a professional."

She was, and she was good at her job, but it was more than that. She saw the same ugliness on the job that he did. She just dealt with it differently.

"You're avoiding," he said.

"You're no better," she replied. "You've got your perfectly sanitized life, your empty office, your disinfected house. You don't even go to church anymore, and I know that you're a Christian. So you tell me—what are *you* avoiding?"

Stewart put the car into gear and pulled out of the drive. He glanced over at Penny, and she met his gaze irritably. He knew her better than she thought, but maybe that went both ways. It wasn't comfortable to have your own issues pointed out.

"Maybe we should stop psychoanalyzing each other," he said.

"Did I get too close to the truth?" she asked.

He turned onto the main road and cast her a rueful look. "Maybe. How about me? Did I get anywhere close to the target?"

"Maybe." She leaned her head against the headrest. "I am curious about why you don't go to church anymore, though."

Stewart sighed. "It's complicated."

"Everything is," she said. "Try me."

He pressed his lips together. This was what *he'd* been avoiding. He liked being the strong one for her but wasn't so keen on opening up himself. Besides, his tangle of emotion and faith wasn't easy to communicate.

"They don't get it," he said. "I guess that's what it comes down to. I go and listen to a sermon where the minister talks about leaving it in God's hands, and having faith that God will work it all out, and…it's no comfort. Not for me. Not when I see the worst of what people are capable of, and the words of comfort are to simply 'leave it to God.' It's my job to fix it, to provide some justice. And then after I do my job, I have to deal with all of those memories in my head. And just leaving it to God? That feels a little trite to me. And like a waste of my Sunday morning."

Okay, that had come tumbling out… He stole a glance in her direction and he found her expression softer.

"So…that's why," he muttered.

"Okay. That's fair."

But Penny did go to church. Somehow, it

worked for her to attend a church and have a faith community in her life. Was he missing something?

"What do you find at church that comforts you?" he asked.

Penny was silent for a couple of beats, and then she said, "You know how when the music is over, and the preacher has started speaking, and you get a ray of sunlight that slants down through a stained-glass window, and you get a piece of dust that just dances there...?"

Stewart tightened his grip on the steering wheel, silent. Yes, he did know how that felt. It made him feel raw and his tears would be too close to the surface to be comfortable.

"That's what I'm looking for at church," Penny continued. "No, the preacher will never understand the horrible things I see at work. In fact, if I unloaded it on him, I'd probably break the poor guy. But that doesn't mean that God isn't real, or that He isn't present, or that He isn't using me to right a few wrongs. And when I see a dust mote dancing in a ray of sunlight that comes pouring in through a stained-glass image of Jesus in Gethsemane, I remember that God is real. And there's something about that feeling of being in a sanctuary full of God's people who all have heavy things in their hearts, and knowing that while none of them understand my burden, they do have burdens of their own. And we're all there looking for a little bit of peace."

Stewart stole a look at her, and her eyes were fixed on the road ahead of them, a slightly wistful look on her face.

"And that's why you go?" he asked.

"That's why I go. I need some comfort. I find it in stained-glass. It reminds me of the God Who still holds us."

"I do believe in God," he said. "Very much. I know He holds us. I know He sustains us..."

"Good." Penny's voice was soft and quiet.

He laughed bitterly. "My mother would

be thrilled to know you're talking me into going to church again."

"Am I talking you into it?" she asked, and his head turned in her direction to find her studying his face.

"You're trying." He shot her a teasing grin.

Penny smiled ruefully and looked away. But his partner had a point. He couldn't expect to be understood by the people there, but he could expect God to understand those burdens he carried. She'd mentioned a stained-glass image of Jesus in Gethsemane. And Jesus had certainly seen the worst that humanity was capable of. Jesus could understand the battered heart of a police detective. It was a good reminder.

SIX

The only hotel on Main Street in Little Dusseldorf was no longer called Slumber Inn. It was now called the Welcome Inn, and when Penny and Stewart asked to speak to the owner, a woman in her thirties came out of an office down a hallway and greeted them with a firm handshake.

"I'm Teresa Balm," she said. "What can I do for you?"

"You're the owner?" Penny confirmed.

"Sure thing. For the last five years."

"We're looking for the previous owner, then," Penny said. "Mike Miller."

"Mr. Miller." Teresa smiled and nodded. "He still comes in for dinner at the restaurant once in a while. He's got a lot of memories here."

"Can we come into your office and chat?" Penny asked.

"Of course."

Teresa led the way back to her office. There was just enough space in the small room for Penny and Stewart to sit side by side, their elbows pressed together in the visitor's chairs in front of Teresa's desk. She had a pile of papers sitting to one end, an open laptop on the desk.

"What do you know about Mike Miller?" Penny asked.

"I know a little bit," Teresa replied. "My husband and I bought this place five years ago, and when we arrived, we were new in Little Dusseldorf. Mike was really well loved, though. He still is, I suppose. Whenever he comes in for a meal, someone always offers to pay for him. People have told us stories about the kind things that Mike has done for them over the years. One woman was a single mother, and he let her bring her son to work with her all summer when he wasn't in school. One man told me that when he was out of work because of an injury, Mike brought him groceries every week, no charge. Things like that."

"Wow." Stewart nodded. "So he was really well-liked."

"Definitely."

"How about the Amish community?" Penny asked. "Did he have a similar reputation with them?"

"Amish folks have paid for his meals, too, but they're more private. They didn't tell me why," she replied.

"Do you know where he is now?" Penny asked.

"He's at the old folks home here in town—Shady Oaks. His granddaughter brings him here for an early dinner sometimes. I think his granddaughter just got married."

Penny jotted down the name in her phone. "Thanks, Teresa. We appreciate your time."

"No problem." Teresa smiled. "Uh…is he okay? Is he in trouble or anything?"

"We're investigating another person he may have known very long ago," Penny replied. "He was reportedly friends with Mike, and we're just trying to get an idea of the sorts of people he spent time with."

"Oh…okay."

Teresa looked less comfortable as Penny and Stewart took their leave. Penny scanned the hotel as they made their way out. It looked like a popular place to eat an early bird dinner, because the attached restaurant was full. So this was the kind of man who had been friends with Caleb. But it sounded like Mike was friendly with the whole community, so perhaps his closeness with Caleb didn't denote anything more than he shared with many others.

Maybe, if Caleb felt like an outsider sometimes in his Amish life, a friendly guy like Mike could help him to feel more like himself again. That was the most generous thought she'd had about her grandfather yet.

An Amish waitress swept past with a

platter of food, and Penny looked longingly after a plate piled high with crisp, golden onion rings.

"Getting hungry?" Stewart asked.

It had already been a long day. They'd been to her mother's place, her uncle's, her grandmother's, had called in some research requests to the station, and were now back in town again. She put a hand on her stomach and felt her face heat. "Yeah, I am. I could use a burger or something."

"How about an actual home-cooked meal?" Stewart asked. "My parents said if we were busy, we should go by their place for dinner one of these days."

"Sure," Penny said. "This isn't too short of notice?"

"They're retired and thrilled to see me whenever they get the chance," he said. "Trust me, they'll be happy to see us."

Penny met her partner's gaze, and a sudden thought occurred to her. This was an opportunity to see elusive, immaculate Stewart with his parents. This was a priceless glimpse into her partner's personal world, and she really couldn't give up the opportunity. He kept wanting her to take a break from work, and this would do nicely. Maybe she could turn her sleuthing on to Stewart instead.

"You mean, you're going to let me see you with your mom and dad?" she asked. "Knowing full well I'm going to ask your mother to show me baby pictures?"

Stewart chuckled. "You wouldn't."

"I might. I haven't decided yet," she countered with a grin.

"I'll take that chance," he said.

"Well, in that case, yes," she said. "Let's do it."

Stewart made a phone call to his mother, spoke briefly with her, and when he was done, he shot Penny a grin.

"Tonight is lasagna," he said. "Let's go."

When they reached the car, Penny saw a long, ugly scratch down the passenger side of the vehicle.

"Someone keyed the cruiser?" Penny said in disbelief. "What about your side?"

"My side is fine," Stewart said, but she saw anger snapping in his eyes. "So we're touching a nerve here somewhere, it would seem. Who's following us?"

"I'd like to know," she said, and they both looked around, scanning for any loiterers who might have witnessed the event. There was no one. And their parking spot wasn't within view of any dashboard cameras, either, which was unfortunate. "Is this supposed to be a message?"

"If it's the same person as the note writer, is this person following us, or just serendipitously running into us?" he asked.

"Either way, they want us to stop," Penny said. "It only makes me more determined."

"They don't know who they're messing with," Stewart said with a short, bitter laugh. "Let's go eat. This can wait, dinner can't."

Then he opened the glove compartment

and pulled out a granola bar and passed it to Penny. "To tide you over."

He knew her so well.

Stewart took over the wheel, and within twenty-five minutes, he pulled into his parents' driveway a little ways outside Lancaster. No one had followed them. Penny had been sure of that.

The house was a cute little bungalow, and lights shone invitingly from the front window. The curtains were open, and Penny saw a man walk across the room. That wasn't safe to leave drapes open so that people from the street could see inside— something she now knew very well from her line of work.

"I always tell them to close those," Stewart said. "They don't listen, though." He looked over at her and gave her a rueful smile.

"This is payback from when you were a teenager and tuned them out," she said with a chuckle.

"Yeah, maybe."

What had Stewart been like as a teenager, she wondered? Maybe she'd get a few clues tonight.

The front door opened before they were even halfway up the walk, and a petite ash blonde woman stood in the doorway with a smile on her face. She had a floral-patterned apron over her clothes, and her face was wreathed in smile lines.

"You made it!" she called. "Welcome, welcome!"

An older man appeared behind her and he waved at them, then they stood back as Penny and Stewart came into the house. Penny could smell cheese and tomato sauce, and her stomach rumbled in response.

"You must be Penny. I'm Sandy." The older woman hustled her in. This would be Stewart's mother, and she could see something of Stewart in her eyes, and in the way she smiled.

"I'm Dan." Dan was tall and well-built,

just like Stewart. And she could see where Stewart got his looks from. Dan and Stew both had the same strong jaw and physique.

"How long have you two been working together and this is the first time we've met you?" Sandy said. "I'm glad he finally brought you by. There's been a standing invitation all this time, you know."

Penny shot Stewart a grin. "All this time, Stew?"

"Do you call him Stew?" Sandy asked with a chuckle. "When he was in grade school, the kids called him Stew."

"When he was in elementary school, he was 'Stewie,'" Dan said. "Then he became Stew in what…grade five? Grade six?"

"And then Stewart when he hit high school," Sandy said.

This was priceless! Penny couldn't help but grin at her partner whose expression had become downright cornered.

"Mom, come on," Stewart said with a laugh. "This is why it took me so long."

"Oh, we aren't embarrassing you, are

we?" Sandy asked. "It's not like you hatched from an egg. You have parents. It's not shocking."

"It isn't," Penny agreed, casting him a teasing smile. "In fact, I think it's great that he has parents who are open and full of stories."

"I'll bet you do…" Stewart muttered and Penny laughed.

"You must be hungry," Dan said. "We've got the meal ready to go. Did you want to come eat now before you get called out? If there's one thing we've learned with Stewart's job, it's that we don't dillydally before serving dinner."

"I really am hungry," Penny said. "Thank you for this. Stew hates how I normally eat. He's a stickler for real food."

"Stewart is a great cook," Sandy said, and she tapped a chair for Penny with a smile. "Have a seat here."

The lasagna was already on the table, and Sandy plucked the tinfoil off the top of the pan, then took the foil off another dish that held sliced garlic bread. This meal looked amazing, and Penny took her seat. Stewart settled opposite her, and his parents took the head and foot of the table. They all bowed their heads and Dan said a blessing.

"Amen," Sandy said. "Stewart, dish up Penny, would you?"

Stewart scooped a big piece of gooey, cheesy lasagna onto Penny's plate, and she accepted a piece of garlic bread from Sandy. Stewart had been right about "real food." This did smell amazing.

"Do you know how to make this?" Penny asked Stewart as she took her first bite.

"Of course," he said, and his gaze met hers with a challenging sparkle.

"Are you serious?"

He shrugged. "A guy has to know how to feed himself."

"You should make her lasagna sometime," Dan said. "It's how I got your mom."

"Did you make this lasagna, Dan?" Penny asked.

"Of course," Dan said with a shrug, but he looked a bit bashful all the same. "Like Stewart says, a man has to know his way around a kitchen. It's how we Miller men woo our women."

Penny chuckled. "Is that true, Stew?"

Because Stewart did seem rather focused on making sure she ate properly, and she felt a strange warmth settle into her middle. Had she been turning down this level of cooking all this time?

"I'm careful who I cook for," Stewart chuckled. "I don't want to make just anyone fall in love with me."

Penny felt some heat hit her cheeks. There might be some truth to that. Falling for Stewart wouldn't be hard. He was a catch, and she knew it.

"Oh, those two!" Sandy said, and she rolled her eyes good-naturedly. "Do you want some salad, Penny?"

"Thanks." Penny dished up the greens onto her plate as well.

"You know, Stewart just thinks the world of you," Sandy said.

"Does he?"

"Yes. He respects your opinions, and he says you're the smartest cop he's ever worked with."

"Wow." Penny's gaze flickered toward Stew, but he had turned toward his father again.

"I've been trying to set him up with women from church," Sandy said, lowering her voice so that their conversation stayed private between the two of them. "Nice and attractive women, but I can't get him to give them a second look. And that's because of you, I think."

"Me?" Penny looked at the older woman surprised. "Oh, I'm not discouraging him from dating! I promise!"

"Oh dear, I don't mean that," Sandy said. "I mean…he sees you every workday, and you're rather hard to compete with. Now that I've met you and seen you two together, I can see it."

The men still seemed engrossed in their own conversation.

"Stew and I would never date," Penny said quietly. "We're colleagues, and very good friends. We'd never play with those lines."

"Is that how you feel?" Sandy asked.

"Stew is...a very, very good friend," Penny admitted. "I've never had anyone I could trust like I trust Stew, and... I've had boyfriends come and go. So, I don't take that stable relationship for granted."

"Good men are hard to find," Sandy agreed softly.

"They are." But Penny didn't want to bare her soul this evening, so she added, "How did you meet Dan?"

"I was twenty-five, and I'd given up," Sandy said. "I was working at a bank and I decided that I would just have to grow old with my cat. Then I went to a different church—I don't remember why—and Dan said hello. It was...different. I can't explain it. We just knew."

"That sounds perfect," Penny said.

"I'd had a few boyfriends come and go, too," Sandy said. "All I can say is that when it's the right guy...he doesn't go."

Yeah, but Penny also knew about Stew's immaculate family history. There was no drama, no abandonment, no murdered grandfathers, stories that left scars on her heart and kept her from opening it to love... Just good people treating each other well. Stewart would eventually meet a woman the same way his parents had met—just stumbling across her one day—and his friendship with Penny would have to change to make room for the woman who would capture his heart. And that was going to hurt a lot—she knew it already. She was already trying to prepare herself for it.

Maybe Penny would grow old with her school of goldfish. She smothered a rueful smile at the thought.

"Here's hoping we all stumble across the right person sooner than later," Penny said.

"I like you a lot," Sandy said with a warm smile. "And even if you never date my son, I think you're good for Stewart. As his work partner, and as his friend. You stretch him a little bit. You make him think about things differently. You make him a little more patient." Sandy took a bite of garlic bread and chewed thoughtfully. "And you keep his interest."

"Do I?" she asked.

"You do."

Sandy didn't enlarge upon that, and Penny was afraid to ask, lest she sound like she was interested in more than a work relationship with Stewart. She wasn't sure that Stewart would forgive her for that, considering how hard his mom was working to find him a girlfriend.

Penny tucked into her meal—both an excuse to stop talking, and because it was delicious and she was hungry. Her partnership with Stewart was a unique and beautiful thing, and it sounded like his mom could see that, too. And Penny would never deny how much Stewart meant to her, but she knew that this beautiful balance was on borrowed time.

Wasn't this the warning she'd grown up hearing over and over again? *Don't lean too much on a man, he might not stick around.*

While friendship might last longer than romance, nothing lasted forever. Things would change eventually, and if she let herself fall for her partner, it would just hurt more than it needed to.

Stewart watched out of the corner of his eye as Penny took her last big bite of lasagna. Was Stewart crazy to have brought her to his parents' place tonight? She and his mom seemed to be having a good chat. But then he heard his mother say something about Renee? That was an ex-girlfriend. He inwardly cringed.

"Mom, really!" he said.

His mother looked up. "It's applicable!"

"To what, exactly?" he asked.

"To what we were talking about. We were talking about relationships, and how it doesn't matter how perfect someone is on paper if they aren't the right person. Like you and Renee."

"Right." He shifted his position, suddenly uncomfortable, and Penny gave him a sympathetic smile. Bringing her here was definitely a bad idea. He'd been wanting to take her somewhere comforting after all the upheavals she'd been enduring, and instead she was getting a whole education into the stuff he didn't talk about.

Stewart finished his plate of food. He loved his dad's lasagna. His father had been perfecting that recipe for decades, and Stewart's lasagna was also pretty good, but it never quite matched his dad's.

"So she doesn't know about your past girlfriends?" his father asked, his voice low.

"Dad, she's not my girlfriend. She's my work partner."

"Yes, but… You're close with her, aren't you? You talk about her all the time."

Stewart glanced across the table and Penny looked over at the same time. Their eyes met, and a smile tickled the corners of her lips. His heart skipped a beat. Yes, they were close… He looked back toward his father.

"I don't like talking about women I've dated with her, okay? It's…not the way I want her to see me."

"Ah." His father nodded. "I get it. You don't want her picturing you with anyone else."

"You make it sound like I'm planning something," Stewart said. But his father was right—he didn't want Penny picturing him with anyone else. He also knew that was out of line. She wasn't his girlfriend. She wasn't a romantic option. She was just… Penny. And he cared about her more than he should.

"I'm not trying to push anything here," his father said. "I'm sorry about that, son.

I'm just trying to get a handle on who she is to you."

She meant more to him than was proper, truth be told, and admitting that wasn't going to be helpful.

"She's my partner. That's it."

"Okay." His father gave a curt nod. "Too bad, though. I like her."

Yeah, so did Stewart. The problem with dating these last few years was that he couldn't fully focus on another woman. Penny was his work colleague, and that was where it was supposed to stop—and where it did stop when it came to his actions—but somehow he couldn't quite move on to someone who might actually be a romantic option, not when he got into a cruiser next to Penny five days a week. His last girlfriend, Renee, had called it quits after a few months of dating, and she'd cited his partnership with Penny as the problem. She said she'd felt like a third wheel to the two of them.

He'd messed up that relationship, and he knew it.

"So…if Penny is just a work colleague, what would you think of meeting one of these women your mother keeps rustling up?" his father asked.

"I don't know, Dad…"

"An introduction goes a long way, you know," his father said. "Maybe you'll like one of them. Maybe you won't. But you don't know until you've met some of them and had a short conversation."

"It's logical, Dad," he agreed, "but I don't know. Maybe we can wait until after this case settles down. It's pretty personal for Penny. This is her grandfather's body we discovered, and it's stirring up a lot of feelings in her family, and for her. She looks tougher than she is. And it's my job to know that. I just need to wait until we're past this. I don't think I could give it my proper attention until then anyway."

"You want to be there for Penny," his father confirmed.

"Yeah, I do."

That covered it. Even if she was "just a colleague," he did want to be there for her. He couldn't leave her dealing with this alone. And by the look on his father's face, he didn't quite buy his claim that Penny was just his work partner. Stewart would have to live with that. Because Stewart knew theirs was a remarkably close relationship, and he couldn't really explain it, either. It was what it was.

When they finished eating, there was a knock at the front door, and Stewart's mother went to answer it. He heard the sound of voices, and his father got up.

"Oh, it's the neighbor's dog," he said. "It won't take us long, but it takes a few of us to corner the little rascal... We'll be back!"

The door slammed shut, and Stewart exchanged a look of mild surprise with Penny. Outside he could hear voices calling a dog named Molly.

"Okay..." he said. "I guess they're chasing a dog."

Penny started to laugh. "Your parents are nothing like I expected!"

"Yeah?" he said. "What did you expect?"

"I don't know... More poise and less personality." She shot him a grin.

"You mean dry as cardboard?" he chuckled. "Much like me?"

Stewart stood up and started piling plates to bring them to the kitchen.

"You are not dry, Stew," Penny said.

"No? I'm all healthy and neat," he said. "That's got to be somewhat boring for you."

"Reliability is not boring." She picked up two serving dishes, and they headed together to the kitchen. "It's nice."

He liked the way she said that. Did she really like his reliability? His heart warmed at that thought. He slid past Penny, lifting the plates as the front of his shirt brushed her shoulder. He didn't want to be set up with other women. What he wanted was this—whatever it was—with Penny. Moments like this one, quiet time together, listening to her talk about her ideas and her thoughts. It wasn't everything he needed, but it was enough that he couldn't let it go, either.

Outside the back kitchen window, he saw a little white-and-brown terrier streak past with four retirees trailing behind. He couldn't help but laugh. Should he help them, he wondered?

He put the plates on the counter and opened the dishwasher.

"So, what have you learned about me so far?" he asked.

"I just have a better image of you growing up. I always knew you had a squeaky-clean family, but now I can understand it better," she replied. "It's less intimidating."

"The idea of my family intimidated you?" he asked.

"A little."

"Why?"

Penny turned toward the window, and Stewart came up behind her, looking at the scene. His parents and their neighbors had the little dog cornered now, and Molly's mistress scooped her up while her master clipped a lead on to her collar. Penny smelled faintly of a sweet perfume that he associated with her almost subconsciously now, and he had to curb the urge to slip an arm around her waist.

"Because they achieved what my family couldn't," she said so quietly, that he almost didn't catch it. "Look at them..."

He followed her gaze out the window to where his father had an arm draped over his mother's shoulder. They were laughing now, and he was struck by how much his parents had aged in the last little while. His father's hair had gone from gray to silver, and his once thick arms were a little more shrunken, too. His mother looked smaller, somehow, and a little frailer.

"How many years have they been married?" Penny asked, and for a moment, they both just stood there watching the older folks outside. Then she turned suddenly. He was standing so close behind her that she almost collided with his chest.

Stewart blinked down at her, and his breath caught. She looked equally surprised, her lips parted, and her eyes widened, and suddenly, all he could think about was closing the last of that distance between them. This wasn't the first time he'd thought about kissing her, but it was the first time he'd considered it while she was close enough to make it happen...

"Uh—forty-five years," he said.

"That's a long time," she whispered.

Stewart didn't know what to tell her, and it was like there was a vacuum where words should be, and to fill it, he reached up and moved a tendril of hair off her forehead. What was it about Penny that drew him in like this?

Bringing her to his parents' place had been a big mistake. It had changed things between them in some unexplainable way. He could feel it.

He heard voices coming closer, and then

footsteps on the patio. He dropped his hand and took a step back just as the back door opened.

"If that Molly weren't so cute—" his mother was saying. "Oh, I'm sorry, Penny. We're used to this. Our neighbor's dog loves to run away into our yard, and we help our neighbors grab her about three or four times a month."

Stewart realized how close he was standing to Penny, and he took a purposeful step back. But that felt wrong, too, being this far from her. What was happening to him? He'd been Penny's partner for three years now, and suddenly he was having trouble with the boundaries?

"I think we have cheesecake in in the basement freezer," Stewart's father said. "Don't we, honey?"

"We do…but it's frozen solid. Do you think we can microwave it to thaw it out?"

"I don't know about that," Stewart said. He had to get them out of here. He needed fresh air, and the comfort of their cruiser.

He had to get them back onto familiar ground again.

His phone rang, and he looked down at the number. It was Nick Adams from the department. He breathed out a sigh of relief. He was pulling a page from Penny's playbook now, leaning back into their work to find some balance.

"I've microwaved cheesecake before," Penny said.

"Somehow, that doesn't surprise me," Stewart said with a teasing smile, and he picked up the call. "Hey, Nick."

"Hi, Stewart. I've got an update for you. You asked us to do a background check on that name change?"

"Yeah, what do you have?" Stewart said, turning away from the kitchen and heading back into the dining room for some quiet. His parents and Penny were still discussing the possibility of microwaving cheesecake.

"Fifty-one years ago, Willard Morrison legally changed his name to Caleb Renno. Caleb Renno's record is squeaky-clean."

"And Willard Morrison's?" Stewart asked.

"Also squeaky-clean. I've got a driver's license, some work history, and that's about it. He was an only child, and obviously both parents are deceased. I did manage to track down a neighbor using the address from his driver's license, and she said she remembered a quiet kid who didn't get into any trouble. Nothing that explains a name change. At least not in the records. I'll keep digging."

Was it witness protection, maybe? Stewart's mind spun ahead.

"Okay, thanks, Nick," he said. "I appreciate it."

When he ended the call, he found Penny and his parents watching him.

"Is there an update?" Penny asked.

"Confirmation on Caleb's name change," Stewart said. "But there's no explanation as to why he did it in the legal paperwork."

"None?" she asked.

"Nothing."

He could see the wheels turning in that

magnificent brain of hers, but it was more than just the case to be solved, the answers to be dug up. This was personal to her, and she needed these answers on a heart level, not just for her thirsty intellectual curiosity. She sobered.

"Actually, Mr. and Mrs. Jones," Penny said, "thank you so much for dinner. It was wonderful to meet you, but I think I'll call it a night and head home."

His parents seemed to understand, because they just nodded, and his father slipped an arm over his mother's shoulder again—that relaxed stance that was so familiar between his parents.

"I'm glad you could make it," his mother said. "You come by anytime and we'll rummage that cheesecake out of the freezer for you."

"Don't tempt me," Penny said with a forced smile, but when her gaze swung back up to meet his, he saw the wariness there. Playtime was over. They were getting back to work.

"I'll drive us," Stewart said.

He was always trying to get her to take a break and unwind, but somehow tonight, he could feel the weight of the problems he couldn't fix. And tonight, he wished he could shoulder a little bit of this burden for her, but he couldn't. This was her grandfather, her family history and her family pain. All he could do was stand by and hope she leaned on him.

SEVEN

The drive back to the city had been a quiet one, and admittedly, Penny was lost in her own thoughts. And it wasn't about her grandfather, either. Stewart hadn't seemed inclined to talk, and she hadn't challenged that. He'd given up a lot of his own personal privacy that evening, and she knew him better now than she ever did before. That had been an enlightening peek into his personal world, and she felt honored to have been allowed into that inner sanctum.

And then there was that moment in the kitchen…that moment before his parents came bursting inside, and Stew's eyes had been so soft, and then he'd touched her face and brushed some hair off her forehead, and she'd thought for just a moment that he was about to kiss her… A trail of goose bumps went up her arms at the memory.

He hadn't kissed her. She hadn't kissed him. They'd just…had a moment. That was all it was, wasn't it? Stewart didn't see her like that, did he? She rubbed her hands over her arms. Goose bumps didn't matter, and she was acting like a silly schoolgirl. He hadn't kissed her. There was nothing to wonder over. Besides, she shouldn't be thinking that way about her partner. They worked together, and they'd always maintained a respectful distance, even if their relationship was close and friendly. He was probably her best friend. Those kinds of relationships were few and far between and she didn't want to do anything to ruin that.

Stewart pulled to a stop in front of the station. The sun had set, and the streetlights had all come on. A crescent moon hung in the dusky sky.

"That was a really delicious meal," Penny said. "Make sure your parents know I really appreciate it."

"I'm glad you enjoyed it," Stewart said. "And they know. Don't worry about it."

Penny put her hand on the door handle, but something held her back. Tonight, the balance had changed between them. That moment in the kitchen—it had blown an ember into something warmer. Things had shifted between her and Stewart. She turned back.

"Are we okay, Stew?" she asked.

"What do you mean?" But she could see the wariness in his expression. He felt it, too. She wouldn't mention the moment in the kitchen. She hadn't processed that enough to even speak about it yet.

"I mean, you and me," she said.

"Of course," he said.

"Are we?" she pressed.

"Yeah, Pen. We're fine." He gave her a small smile—the familiar kind she was so used to. The kind of smile that always brought her feet right back down to earth again.

"Maybe it's just this case. I'm not my-self," she said.

"It's okay. I get it. This has been a lot for you."

"Am I too personally involved?" she asked, her voice low.

"Probably," he said with a nod.

She could count on Stew to just say it straight. She *was* too close to this...

"Are you going to report that?" she asked.

Because he should. Stewart pressed his lips together. She could feel him weighing his words.

"Do you need to dig this up, even if it hurts?" he asked at last.

"I really do. And I have a feeling it's going to hurt. It's going to change a lot for our family, too. But that can't be avoided. The truth is the truth, and I need to find it. It'll kill me to just sit back and let someone else dig into our history and come to their own conclusions."

Stewart nodded a couple of times, then shrugged.

"Then, no, I won't report it," he said. "You're human, Pen. You have emotions. And this is a cold case. There are no recent victims, no worry about a re-offense... I mean, there's someone who'd rather we didn't look into it, but they'll just have to live with it. We're going to get answers."

"Thank you." She meant that more deeply than he probably realized.

"I care." His voice was a deep rumble that tugged at her. "I really do."

And the way his gaze softened, it sounded like he was saying more than the words relayed. But she felt it, too.

"I know," she said, and she dropped her gaze. She didn't know what this was building between them. It was a rawer, more intimate version of their partnership, but she didn't know what that even meant. To him. To her.

"I'm going to head home and get some rest," Penny said. "We can get back at it in the morning."

"Okay. That's a good idea," he replied.

And maybe by morning, she'd feel more like herself again, because she was wanting to lean on Stew more than she had any business doing. And while she wished she could blame it on this case, she didn't think that was root of it... This had been growing for a while, and this case was making it harder to ignore.

Penny headed over to her own vehicle and drove home. She made her way up to her condo and let herself inside. Her fish tank glowed softly from the corner of her living room, and she flicked on lights and headed over to look into the tank. Her goldfish swam in lazy circles, and she sprinkled some fish food on top of the water.

Then she sank into the center of her couch and lowered her face to her hands. She felt tired...so very tired.

"Lord, I feel like everything is coming apart," she whispered.

Her close, no-nonsense relationship with her partner was starting to feel more vulnerable. The family story she'd known all her life was unravelling, too. *Dawdie* Caleb wasn't the cad who'd left his family after all. And he wasn't even Caleb! He was a man with a hidden history. Would she discover that Caleb was worse than she'd ever believed? Or would she forgive him?

Caleb was a man long dead. He'd gone to meet his Maker forty-eight years ago. What was it about a family tree that connected its members this way? Caleb shouldn't matter, and yet she was realizing that he had formed their family long after he vanished. Their memories of him, their assumption, their fears, their heartbreak, had all been influenced by the loss of one man.

He'd mattered a great deal to his wife, and to his children. His absence had affected his children's lives. Sarah had gone through two painful divorces, and Penny could see how her father's supposed abandonment of the family had played into both of them. Sarah had expected a man to leave. She'd feared it. She'd hoped to avoid it, and then she'd gone about setting up her life so that if the man she loved left her, she'd be okay. And each husband had inevitably left. If she had expected something different, would she have chosen differently in her romances? Would she have behaved differently within those relationships?

Penny didn't blame her mother, but she did blame Caleb. Or she had until she realized he'd been dead all that time, not simply living it up with a new family. So who was to blame now?

And was Penny any different than her mother? If Caleb's disappearance had so deeply influenced his children that their deepest fears played out again and again, how deeply was Penny influenced by it all? She had her own misgivings about the longevity of romantic relationships. She was careful, and tried not to expect too much from a relationship, and she normally wasn't disappointed in that. Her boyfriends moved along after a few months.

"Lord, I need your help," she prayed. "I

need to know who Caleb was. I suppose I need to know if he was a good man…or a forgivable one. Give me the strength to face the truth and get my balance back. Give me the strength…"

An image of Stewart rose in her mind—with his gentle gaze, and his strong hands, standing stalwartly by her side. But that was too tempting…too easy to rely on him, and he was only her partner. She needed to keep that completely clear in her own mind.

"Not him, Lord," she whispered. "I'm teetering on the edge of falling in love with my partner. I'm going to need my own strength this time around." She couldn't bear the thought of not having Stewart in her life, of him leaving her. If they took the relationship into romantic territory, she knew the timeline. A few months, and he'd be done with her, too. He meant too much to her, and what they had now was just fine, something stable and dependable. She didn't want to risk losing that.

Then Penny flicked on the TV, found an old Ingrid Bergman movie, and pulled an afghan over her legs. She just needed a little comfort tonight.

The next morning, Penny woke up feeling rested and renewed. A solid night's sleep could do wonders for a woman's perspective. She went to the station, parked in her regular spot and headed inside. When she passed Stewart's office, he silently held out a mug of taupe coffee as he always did. This would be her third coffee of the day, but she always appreciated it. She accepted the mug with a grateful smile and carried it on down to her own office.

Penny went inside and sank onto her office chair, then pulled out her phone where she had a running list of people to question.

There were several family members still living she could talk to about that night, but right now, they didn't interest her. Nick had managed to get more information on Willard Morrison, before the name change—an old friend named Henry who'd attended the same high school. He said he wasn't surprised that Willard had turned Amish since he'd always been looking for deeper meaning in life. Henry had been a churchgoer and had invited Willard to youth events a few times, but nothing had stuck.

The one person who topped Penny's personal list was Caleb's very close *Englisher* friend, Mike Miller. Family had a way of remembering the story of the night Caleb disappeared—the way they'd always relayed it—and memories could be altered through repetition. They'd told each other the same tale time and time again, trying to make sense of what happened and come to a consensus about why he'd left. But Mike might remember that night differently…at least, she was hoping so.

"I just got a text from the excavation site," Stewart said, coming into her office.

"Did they find something else?" she asked.

"They did." He held up his phone and she could see what looked like a badly tarnished piece of jewelry. "An earring, they think."

"An earring?" Penny squinted, looking at it photo again. "The Amish don't wear jewelry."

"I know."

"So whose is it? The killer's?"

"Maybe? You know as much as I do now," Stewart replied. "But I think we should head back to the well and take a look ourselves. It's weird, and it has to be connected."

Penny grabbed her mug of coffee—it was drinkably warm now—and took three big gulps.

"If we're going to be in the area, I think we should swing by the local precinct and check into Officer Robbie, too," she said.

"Good idea," he agreed. "Let's go."

Last night, this had all felt too emotionally heavy, but maybe a new clue was what she needed after all. Focusing on the puzzle was so much easier than focusing on her grandfather. Maybe *this* was the answer to her prayer.

Stewart couldn't help but smile as Penny strode past him and pushed open the door that led to the parking lot. She had a spring in her step again, and she looked like she'd gotten some of her balance back. He was glad to see her looking more like herself.

"Penny," he said, and she turned.

He tossed the cruiser keys to Penny and she caught them midair.

"And they didn't find anything else?" Penny asked.

They headed out to their cruiser. Penny hit the key fob and unlocked the doors.

"Not yet," Stewart said. "But they're still digging out the shale at the bottom of the well, so maybe there will be more by the time we get there."

"So far, we've got my grandfather's remains, and an earring," she said, pulling open the driver's side door. "That's not a lot to go on. We don't even know if the earring is connected or was lost or thrown there before this happened."

"We'll figure it out," Stewart said with more confidence than he felt. "At least we're still coming up with new evidence, right? That's more than can be said about a lot of cold cases."

He got into the passenger side and did up his seat belt. Penny did up hers, too, then looked over at him.

"My grandfather might have been a worse man than we even thought. He might have been hiding from the law, or from justice. He might have been using my grandmother and the whole, good-hearted Amish community."

"Maybe," Stewart agreed. "It could have been witness protection…"

"But from what? He's not listed as a witness in any big cases. There's no evidence so far that he was involved in any illegal activity. None of this makes sense. Every theory is just such a stretch to make it fit."

Stewart just shook his head. "Let's go check out the latest evidence. Eventually it will all click into place."

It would have to, because Penny wouldn't stop until it did. He knew that much.

When they arrived in town, they swung by the local precinct first and sat down with the commander of the station who pulled out their records. There was only one officer from that time period who'd had the first name Robert, and his picture showed a round faced, freshly shaven man with a boyish smile. By the time he retired, he was Sergeant Robert Fuller, and he'd both climbed in his career and had retired early. No big complaints about him. No big commendations, either. Just a cop who did his job. It might be a similar career history for Penny when she finally retired, or Stewart, too, for that matter.

"Is Robert Fuller still alive?" Penny asked.

"Sure is. He's actually staying at Shady Oaks here in town."

The Shady Oaks Retirement Lodge was where Mike Miller was staying, too. With all the retirement communities in this area, that would make the investigation a little easier.

They thanked the commander for her time and headed back out to their cruiser.

"Do you think he's connected?" Penny asked.

"At this point, nothing would surprise me," Stewart replied. "I wouldn't mind having a chat with him soon, though."

"Caleb had some strange friendships," Penny said thoughtfully.

"Let's head out to your grandmother's place now," Stewart said. "I want to get a close-up look at that earring. It's some actual evidence at long last."

And Penny had to agree. Some concrete evidence besides the body was not to be taken for granted after forty-eight years.

When they arrived at the excavation site,

they found the team still sifting through crumbled clay that was being brought up from the bottom of the well. The shards of hard dirt lay on filtering screens, and techs were softening it with water as they worked through every inch.

"You made it," Nick Adams said, rising to his feet. He went to a bin and pulled out a sealed, clear plastic bag, and brought it to them.

Stewart accepted the bag and turned it over in his hands. There was a rather large dangle earring that appeared to be made of red and clear gems. Rubies and diamonds, if the stones were real. The earring had two joints—one of which was broken, and the other was almost destroyed, but he could see what the earring had looked like in its day. The first stone at the post appeared to be a ruby. The dangling sections were made up of smaller white and red stones encrusting tear drop shapes. If it was costume jewelry, it was well-made. If it was real, it would be worth a lot.

He passed it over to Penny, and she turned it over in her hands thoughtfully.

"This wouldn't have belonged to an Amish person," she said. "Obviously."

"It's obviously connected," Stewart agreed. "Too coincidental. And it's incredibly formal. I mean, unless he was murdered by a woman in evening wear, I doubt that this was worn by the killer."

"True," she said. "How far down was it found, Nick?"

"Two inches," Nick said. "But if there was any water in the bottom, it could have sunk in the silt."

Penny nodded slowly.

"Think we should ask your grandmother if it's familiar?" Stewart asked.

"We can ask, but I doubt it will be. She's Old Order Amish, Stew."

Penny's understanding of the Amish ways was helpful, but her view of her grandmother was a blind spot for her.

"She was married to a man who used to be *English*," he replied. "Sometimes adults hide things from the younger generation for a reason. She might have information she hasn't disclosed yet…or they might simply be things she didn't think were connected to Caleb's death."

Penny met his gaze for a beat, then nodded.

"You're right," she replied.

"I'm going to take over custody of this evidence for a few minutes," Stewart said, turning to Nick. Nick handed him the clipboard and Stewart signed his name next to the item on the sheet of paper that would track the evidence's chain of possession. He'd return it when he was done, but he found that a physical item tended to have more power to rattle a person than a simple picture, and if Elizabeth recognized the earring, he wanted to see it in her reaction.

Penny would want to calm her grandmother, and Stewart wanted the opposite. Rattled people told the truth a lot more easily than calm people did.

They left the excavation site together,

walking down a now well-worn path that led out to the farmhouse yard. The trees rustled in a passing wind overhead, and Stewart looked down at the earring again.

Was it real? That was his most pressing question. Was this some good-quality costume jewelry that had held up well over time, was it a well-made piece of lower priced jewelry using gold and glass, or was this the real thing?

Elizabeth opened the door when they knocked, and she ushered them in with a smile.

"Penny!" Elizabeth said with a tired smile. "I'm glad to see you. How is your mother?"

Elizabeth seemed to be in a good mental space today—alert and aware. That would be useful.

"She's in one piece, but she's pretty shocked. I think the news that her father was murdered has really shaken her."

"*Yah, yah…*" Elizabeth murmured. "I knew she would be upset. So am I. I wish she'd come see me. Some things need to be dealt with together, as a family. Alone, we get lost in the tangle."

"You could go see her," Penny suggested.

"I could hire a van," Elizabeth said. "It's a little more difficult for me to get to her, I confess. The problem is, Sarah doesn't have a community to help her sort things out."

"She has me, *Mammi*," Penny said. "And she does go to church."

"Church for you and church for me mean two different things," the old woman retorted, but she beckoned them in as she talked. "For you, church is a place you go on Sunday. You say hello, you listen to a sermon, and you go home. Am I right?"

Elizabeth fixed her demanding gaze onto Stewart.

"That's how it works," Stewart agreed.

"Well, church for us Amish folks means something different. We are the church. Us, together. We don't even have a church building. We meet in each other's homes each week, and we take turns hosting.

Because church is *not* a building, it's our community. We help each other, support each other, remind each other of who we are. And when hard times come, you have people who know you through and through to help you."

Stewart folded his hands in front of him. He wasn't about to be sidetracked by arguments with Penny's grandmother. That wasn't why they were there.

"For some people, we need a little more privacy with our pain," Penny said.

"No, you *want* more privacy with your pain. You *need* community. That's the difference. You want what is bad for you, like a child craving sweets," Elizabeth said, then sighed. "Sarah knows better—I raised her with community. You, dear girl, weren't raised with it, so I can understand your perspective a little better. My daughter has less excuse!"

Stewart met Penny's gaze and she gave him a wan smile.

The kitchen was clean, except for a few

pots in the sink. A pile of mail sat on the edge of one counter, and he used the tip of a pen to move a few envelopes. It looked like two personal letters, and a bill from a pharmacy. Nothing surprising.

"Here I am spouting off about community, and I haven't even fed you. Forgive me, Stewart. Can I get you something to eat?" Elizabeth asked, her tone softening.

"No thank you, ma'am," he replied with a smile. "I appreciate the offer, though. We're actually here on some official business."

"Are you now?" Elizabeth's smile faltered. "Here I thought it was a visit. Is there news?"

"We wanted to show you something we found in the well and see if it is familiar to you." Stewart pulled the evidence bag from his pocket and held it out so that she could look at the earring on the flat of his hand. Elizabeth stared at the earring, then frowned.

"That's not Amish," she said.

"I know," he said. "But it was down in the well. Do you recognize it?"

"Inside the well?" Elizabeth asked.

"Yes, ma'am."

"With my husband?"

"Yes, ma'am. Do you recognize it?"

"No," Elizabeth replied, but her hands shook. "We don't wear things like that. It's fancy. We are plain people, and something like that would go against our *Ordnung*... that's our rules. Maybe Penny could explain."

"I already did, *Mammi*," Penny said. "But we were wondering if maybe you'd seen it before somewhere."

"No, no, I haven't. I think I'd remember that," Elizabeth said. "People around here don't have jewelry."

"What about *Englisher* friends?" Stewart asked. "Did anyone's wife have earrings like these?"

Elizabeth shook her head. "I didn't know that many *Englishers*. My husband was the one who chatted with them, and he always talked with the men. That was how we did things—properly. Amish men don't just chat with women, you see." Her eyes clouded. "But a woman's earring in our well?"

Penny moved closer to her grandmother's side. "We don't know why it was there yet, *Mammi*."

"I just finished thanking *Gott* that my husband hadn't left me and that Caleb was a good man after all! And now I find out that there was a woman's earring with him in that well... What does that mean about my husband, Stewart?"

"I don't know, ma'am," he said quietly.

"Was he...was he...stepping out on me?" Elizabeth's voice shook. "I shouldn't care. I shouldn't! All these years I assumed he had done just that. And then I got this heartbreaking hope that maybe he'd loved me truly after all...to lose it again?"

Stewart felt a well of guilt. This was the job—dig until they got answers—but he hated leaving people in emotional turmoil because of his questions.

"*Mammi*, I'm going to make some tea," Penny said. "Why don't we all sit down together and talk?"

Stewart went over to the table and pulled a chair out for Elizabeth, then took a seat in the one next to it. Elizabeth sank into the proffered chair.

"Tea might help," she agreed, her voice trembling.

There was no way they could leave Elizabeth alone after this kind of shock. However people explained it, or lived it out, they needed each other. Elizabeth needed someone to talk to about her questionable late husband. Penny needed some family support and perspective as she grappled with her questionable grandfather.

Maybe there was a part deep inside of Stewart that needed this connection, too. And watching Penny stoke up the woodstove and put a teapot on a burner, he felt a wave of comfort that he knew had nothing to do with an Amish kitchen or the elderly woman who owned it. The comfort he felt was all about Penny.

EIGHT

Penny and Stewart only left her grand-mother's home when a cousin came by to check on Elizabeth. And while Penny had been eager to get outside into some fresh air, she felt a tug of guilt. None of this was her fault, but being the bearer of that kind of news came with its own responsibility. She needed to solve this case for her grand-mother's sake, as well as her own.

Penny went down the wooden steps and headed numbly toward the cruiser. She opened the door and sank into the passen-ger seat, heaving a sigh. For a moment, Stewart just sat there in the driver's seat, the keys in his hand, then he looked over at her.

"Are you okay?" he asked.

"Of course."

Because she'd done this before, hadn't she? She'd sat down with a widow or the child of the deceased, and she'd quietly outlined the facts. People needed facts— they'd find comfort to cushion those sharp, painful facts later—but the truth mattered.

"No, it's not something that's a given, Pen," Stewart said. "That was pretty intense in there. That's difficult for anyone— including you. You aren't made of steel. You're a flesh-and-blood woman—I know that, even if you try to pretend otherwise. So I'm going to ask you again. Are you okay?"

Penny's heart fluttered in her chest and she licked her lips. She'd meant to just pack this away, to shove it down to a safe, deep part of her heart to look at later when she felt stronger. But that wasn't going to work, was it?

"Um…not completely," she admitted.

Stewart reached out and took her hand. His warm, calloused grip closed over hers, and she squeezed back hard, trying to keep the tears on the inside. Because he was right—this was harder than she'd ever imagined it would be.

"What do you need?" he whispered.

"Just to sit here for a minute…"

He settled back in his seat, and his grip on her hand loosened, but he didn't release her, either. His thumb moved soothingly over the top of her hand.

"Do you want to stay here with your grandmother and I can take it from here?" he asked.

Penny shook her head. "No, I want to dig and get some answers. I can't make her feel any better with platitudes, can I?" She was silent for a moment. "What if he's worse than we thought?"

"Then…you'll make your peace with it," he said.

"Will she, though?" Penny asked. "Will my grandmother be able to make her peace with it?"

"She's imagined the worst for years," he

replied. "I can promise you that. When a spouse up and leaves, the one left behind has to go through all those what-ifs…and she's lived with a thousand possibilities all this time. I think knowing which one was true would be a relief."

Stewart was right, of course. Penny nodded. "Okay, so what's the next step in the investigation?"

"I have no idea what connection the earring has," Stewart said. "But we do know approximately where your grandfather lived before he became Amish, right? We've got an address, and it's a rural area near Pittsburgh. So I say we head back to the station and start looking up cases that happened around that area within a year or so of the time your grandfather changed his name. We've looked for big cases that might have landed him in witness protection, but maybe it's smaller. If something scared him, I think we can find it."

That sounded logical, and she was al-

ready feeling stronger and more pulled together as he outlined their plan.

"Okay," she said. "I agree. But first I
want to get in front of a storyboard and
put everything together. I need to see it all
in one place."

Stewart gave her hand one more squeeze,
and then he let go. Was it just her, or did
he seem reluctant to release her fingers?
Or maybe it was her reluctance… She felt
some heat touch her cheeks, and the seat
creaked beneath her as she straightened.

Stewart was so easy to lean on these
days, and her first instinct seemed to be
to come to him with her difficulties. And
he seemed to be welcoming it! But if she
let herself lean on him too much, she knew
that her heart would follow, and that would
only complicate their work relationship…
and her own equilibrium.

Back at the station, Penny stood at a
whiteboard in her office, writing down
what they had so far, with a squeaking

erasable marker. She listed the clothing found with the victim, the cause of death, his legal name and the date he changed it to Caleb Renno. In another list, she put down the people they knew for certain were present at the time of his disappearance.

Sometimes seeing everything together in black-and-white could make it clearer in her mind. Stewart leaned against the edge of her desk, his arms crossed over his chest, and she glanced back at him.

"Am I forgetting anything?" she asked.

"The rumor that he left in a car," he replied.

"Right." She jotted that down at the bottom, then exhaled slowly. This was it—the information they had so far.

"Why did he become Amish?" Stewart murmured.

"Hmm?" She turned.

"Why Amish?" Stewart asked. "He wasn't raised Amish. He was just a regular American guy, and he decided to change his faith, his way of life, everything."

"Becoming Amish is a very big commitment," she agreed. "But this is Pennsylvania. A lot of people have Amish connections. We go out to Amish country for some relaxation. I'm pretty confident that most people have Amish-made items in their homes. It isn't like the Amish faith is hidden around here."

"True, but if he was choosing a faith, why one that's so difficult to join?"

"According to my grandmother, the language barrier wasn't difficult for him to overcome," she replied. "But you're right. Why?"

"Who would know?" he asked.

"In order to join the faith, he'd have to go to the bishop of the community," Penny said. "The bishop and the elders would make sure he understood what he was getting himself into, and would have to be convinced of his sincerity before allowing him to be baptized into the faith."

"Which, apparently, they did," he said.

"It would seem," she said. "As for why he

did it, and why they allowed him to join, the only one to ask would be the bishop."

"Is he around still?" Stewart asked.

"No, he's dead. I know that because I remember when they got their new bishop. It was a very big deal in the community because the new bishop was a little more forward-thinking than the last one. He allowed telephones in the barns."

"How long ago?" he asked.

"About ten years."

"So that's not going to help us," he said. "I wonder if there might be some living elders who remember."

"Maybe, but the elders tend to be older men in the community. We can try, of course, but they will most likely have passed away by now."

Somehow, sorting through all of the details with Stewart felt like it was starting to bandage over her raw feelings.

Her office phone rang and Penny picked up the call.

"Detective Moore," she intoned.

"Leave it alone…" a gravelly voice said.

Penny immediately hit the speaker button so that Stewart could hear, too.

"What are you talking about?" she asked.

"You know what I'm talking about. It was a long time ago. If you don't want to create fresh problems for yourself, drop the case."

"Who are you?" she asked.

"Someone who knows who you are. I know where you live. I know what your car looks like. And I blend in very nicely on any city street. Drop it."

The line went dead, Penny's heart hammered to a stop, and Stewart immediately strode to the door, flung it open and called out, "Trace that call that came to Detective Moore's office!"

"On it," the receptionist replied.

When Stewart came back into the office, Penny's heartbeat had started to slow again.

"If he dare come anywhere near you—" Stewart started.

"He called the station," Penny said. "Not my cell phone. He doesn't have as much information as he claims. I think he's just trying to rattle us."

"Well, he succeeded," Stewart said.

"This doesn't make sense!" Penny rubbed her hands over her face. "Whoever killed Caleb is either dead or elderly. That was a young man's voice. Who cares this deeply forty-eight years after the fact?"

"That's what I want to know," Stewart said. "I'm going to laugh if that person was dumb enough to use a cell phone to call us."

A moment later the receptionist poked her head into the office. "I called the phone company. That last call was placed at..." She read out the phone number. "It's a pre-paid phone."

Penny sighed. Not as dumb as they'd hoped. "A burner phone. Great."

But they were still irritating someone. But who? And what avenues were getting too close for comfort?

"Why me?" Penny asked suddenly. "Why not you?"

"Someone knows about your connection?" Stewart suggested. "This is your grandfather's murder after all. Your name might be the only one they know."

"So…someone without police connections," she said.

"That would by my guess."

"How safe is my grandmother, if they're trying to intimidate me?"

"Hold on—" Stewart headed for the door again, and when he returned he said, "The chief says they'll get some units stationed at your grandmother's house to watch for anything suspicious."

"I'm calling my mother," she said. "She can go stay with *Mammi* tonight. I don't want to leave her alone."

Penny made the call and her mother immediately started packing an overnight bag. Between Sarah and her siblings, they could arrange to make sure that *Mammi* wouldn't be alone again until this case was wrapped up.

After Penny finished, she and Stewart just looked at each other, both of their minds spinning through the recent events, then Penny sighed, pulled off the lid of her dry erase marker and jotted the phone call details onto the whiteboard.

"What do we do? Do we try and chase down a burner phone, or keep digging into the case?" Stewart asked, taking the top off a file storage box.

Most files had been digitized at this point, but the smaller precincts didn't have the manpower to do every file and every case back this far. They'd had these overnighted to them. That box contained files on all crimes committed in the jurisdiction surrounding Willard Morrison's home. He pulled out a thick pile of folders and held them out.

"Let's dig," Penny said, and she accepted the records and sank into a chair. As long as she knew her grandmother was safe, she needed to crack this case.

The hours slipped by as Penny flipped through file after file of crimes committed. There were some thefts, a fair number of domestic violence cases, some drunk-and-disorderly charges… Nothing that stood out. There was a rather large case involving organized crime and the theft and transport of a large number of vehicles to other states, but that case was wrapped up, charges were laid, sentences were handed down, and Willard Morrison's name didn't appear anywhere on the witness lists.

"Finding anything interesting?" Penny asked.

Stewart looked up. He sat with one foot on his knee, a folder open as he flipped through the pages inside. He slowly shook his head.

"This one is the theft of a motorcycle," he said. "You?"

She tossed him the file with the organized crime ring. It was thick.

"This is all I've got," she said, "but it doesn't look like it's going to connect to Willard Morrison."

Penny stood up to stretch her back and she wandered over to the window, looking outside at the parking lot. It wasn't much of a view, but it helped to give her eyes a rest. Then she went back to the box and looked inside. There were a few files left, and she pulled them out.

The first folder was another drunk and disorderly. The second was a missing person's case for a teenaged girl, but she'd been found in Pittsburgh later on, robbing a liquor store. So that wasn't a happy ending. Penny hoped the girl had eventually pulled her life together.

The last file made her pause, though, and she frowned.

"You have something?" Stewart asked.

"It's a robbery in Little Dusseldorf." She flipped through the pages, her gaze scanning past the evidence. "An antique store."

"But that's where Caleb moved to, not

where he was running from—if he was running," Stewart said. "So I'm not sure it applies."

"It's a little too coincidental to dismiss, though. They never found the perp, and the robbery was committed a few months before Caleb, or Willard, whatever we want to call him, was killed."

"Maybe it is connected and we need to work backwards?" Stewart said.

"Maybe." Penny looked through the papers she had. "This isn't the full file. There's got to be more."

"I wish they had all this scanned and available online," Stewart muttered. "But this was a local PD case. They might have more information at the local station. Who's got jurisdiction over Little Dusseldorf?"

Penny flipped through the pages until she saw it listed. "Trent River. That's a bigger town about ten miles away from Little Dusseldorf. We could go down there and see what files they still have. It's a long shot, but it's the only lead we've got."

But still, a lead was a lead, and there was something about this case that tickled at her instincts. It was far too coincidental to be nothing. She could feel it.

Trent River PD was small, neat and run with army precision. Stewart and Penny spent most of the afternoon going through their records room, which was a small room in the basement lined with boxes that had been labeled with dates in permanent marker. They went through two cartons that might have held the case they were looking for without finding anything useful. Stewart rubbed his hands over his face.

"Tired?" Penny asked.

Stewart looked over to find Penny watching him, and he smiled wanly.

"Yeah," he said. "You?"

Penny just shrugged, but then she didn't admit to being tired too often. She was stubborn that way. He rose and went over to where she stood, then leaned against the wall next to her.

"Isn't it strange that there could be a robbery in a small town like Little Dusseldorf, and never find the one who did it?" Penny asked, but her attention was still on the box she was going through. She pulled out a new file.

"I don't know," he replied. "These things happen."

"But think about it—a sudden leap in financial freedom—wouldn't that be noticeable? Everyone knows each other. Everyone's in everyone else's business. You'd think they'd notice someone's financial circumstances changing right after a robbery. Besides, one of your own has been robbed, has lost what was rightfully theirs. Isn't there a community desire to see the thief caught?"

"Unless the person who carried out the robbery lived in a very uniform way within a community that made a point of living simply," he replied and raised one eyebrow.

"You mean if the thief was Amish." She didn't sound offended, though. Just thoughtful.

"It would make hiding in plain sight a whole lot easier," he replied. "If anyone knows how to blend in, it's an Amish person."

"It's possible," she agreed. "So let's look at what we have so far. An antique store is robbed overnight. Only a few things were taken, but nothing itemized here. We're going to need the rest of the file. There was a video camera, but the cord wasn't properly covered with a conduit outside the building and was cut so there was no footage. The owner had three employees, all family members, and none appeared to have any extra influx of money."

"So it's likely someone who didn't work there," he said.

"But someone who knew the shop well enough to cut the camera wire," Penny murmured.

They fell into silence, and Penny dropped

the file back into the box and leaned against the wall next to him.

"Can I ask you something?" Penny said quietly.

"Of course."

"Am I messed up?"

Stewart blinked at her and straightened. "What?"

"I'm serious," Penny didn't look at him, though. Her gaze stayed fixed on the linoleum floor in front of them. "You know me better than anyone. Do I carry around a lot of personal baggage?"

"What makes you think that?"

"I'm thirty-four and still single. I'm too cautious, I'm told. I work too much. I'm guarded. I certainly don't have the life I dreamed of."

Was she unhappy? That had never occurred to him before. He knew how much she loved her job, and she was an excellent detective. But in the last three years working shoulder to shoulder with Penny, he'd never thought to question if she was satisfied. Or happy. He'd assumed she was.

"What life did you dream of?" he asked.

"Marriage. Kids. Love." She shrugged. "Career, too, of course. But I always thought I'd have the rest. It hasn't happened."

"I'm pretty sure you could snap your fingers and have about fourteen eligible guys lined up," he said with a low laugh. She was gorgeous, smart, interesting, successful.

"I'm not as certain about that," she said.

"Okay…maybe two or three, though." He sobered. "If you set my mother on it, she'd add a few more to that number."

She chuckled softly.

"Where is this coming from?" he asked.

"I've been thinking for a while," she said, "is this really the life I want? Or is this the life I aimed at because I was scared to really go for what I wanted?"

"You don't want to be a cop?" he asked cautiously.

"Oh, I want to be a cop," she said. "But maybe I don't want to be lonely."

Lonely… That word stabbed under his defenses. He spent every day with her, and she was still lonely? Maybe he wanted to be the one to fill that one need for her— be the one who heard her when she talked, and made her feel understood.

"Being single doesn't make you messed up," he said. "I'm just as single as you are. Am I messed up?"

She looked over at him then, but he saw the teasing twinkle in her eye.

"Kind of." Penny leaned closer, nudging his arm with her shoulder to show that she was joking. It brought her in so close that he could see a stray eyelash on her cheek, and he reached up to brush it away.

But as he touched her cheek, he found his gaze moving over the faint freckles on her nose, and a wave of tenderness crashed over him.

"You're not messed up," he said quietly. "You're careful because you know it's dangerous out there. You're a little reserved, but that just means that your heart is a bigger gift. When a guy is blessed enough to get your heart, he'll know he earned it."

The teasing smile evaporated from her face, and she froze as if holding her breath. He could see her pulse fluttering at the base of her neck, and his own breath caught, too.

"What guy?" she whispered. "I don't have them lining up, Stew."

Me. The realization was like a kick to the gut. He wanted to be that guy who she trusted enough to open to. He wanted to be the one who earned her heart...

Blast. That wasn't wise, was it?

But there she was, looking up at him with that question in her eyes—wondering who on earth would see her like he did, and if he answered her, he'd say too much, so he did the only other thing he could think of right now—the only thing that could keep him from saying exactly what he felt—and he lowered his lips over hers.

At first she stiffened, then she leaned

into his kiss. He held her hand still, and he didn't dare pull her into his arms. For a moment, everything around them melted away—the boxes, the florescent light, the tabletop, the linoleum floor... It was just him and Penny, and this one stolen kiss that he knew he'd regret later, but for the life of him, he couldn't break off.

Footsteps sounded outside the door, and Penny pulled back first, her fingers fluttering up to her lips. He pressed his lips together and closed his eyes.

"Pen, I'm sorry I—"

Then the door opened and a young officer poked her head inside.

"We think we found the file you were looking for," she said. "It was in a pile on Officer Duncan's desk. He's on vacation right now."

Stewart accepted the file from the woman's hands and he opened it. The file was for a robbery case. The Little Dusseldorf Antique Shop.

"This is it," he said.

Stewart headed over to a small table and put the folder down, pulling out sheaves of paper. "The Little Dusseldorf Antique Shop. A robbery done at night..."

He looked over at the officer and shot her a grin. "Thank you. We appreciate it. This is just what we needed. What was he doing with it?"

"Some local history buff was looking into it. We don't have that much crime around here, so... I guess this was interesting for him."

"Thanks."

"Glad to help," she said, and she disappeared out the door again, her footsteps resounding up the stairs.

Penny slipped in next to him, and the soft scent of her perfume slid around him. She picked up a bundle of papers that were stapled together and flipped through them. It was like they were playing at detective—putting up a good show of earnest professionalism that he didn't feel right now. Stewart looked down at her, waiting, and after a moment, she looked up, her cheeks touched with pink.

He didn't know what to say… He'd just kissed her for the very first time, and he wasn't sure if she was going to be angry with him, or if this just complicated their relationship.

"She's gone," he said.

"I know." She lifted her chin—a show of defiance, and she put the papers back on the table. "She almost saw that."

"Yeah, and it's not ideal, but we're both adults."

"I don't need rumors running around about me, Stew."

He swallowed and nodded. "I hadn't thought of that. I'm sorry I kissed you."

The color in her cheeks deepened. "You don't need to apologize."

"You sure?" he asked. Because if she made him apologize, it might be easier—give him a kick in the pants and make him never consider kissing her again. Because right now, all he could think about was the softness of her lips and the way her breath had felt against his face.

"We probably shouldn't do that again, though," she said.

He smiled ruefully. "Probably not. It's... a bit complicated."

"A bit."

What he wanted to tell her was how long he'd been wanting to do that, and how of all the men she could date, none of them would see her quite the way he did. She could find a good guy—he was sure of it—but no one knew her like he did. No one could.

Penny nodded to the file. "This is less complicated. Let's just...focus on work right now."

Was that rejection? Because it wasn't like he went around kissing women on a trial basis or something. But he didn't know what he was wanting from her, either. She deserved a great guy, but she was also his complete opposite. She threw herself into work, and he looked for balance.

He normally looked for balance. He had no idea what he was doing today!

"Okay," Stewart said, and he forced his attention back to the file.

"What do we have?" she asked.

"I've got a list of typical items sold at the antique shop. Not very expensive stuff. And then there's this—the only items stolen."

He picked up a photocopy of a picture—it was grainy and black-and-white, but the necklace and earrings were clear enough, and his heartbeat sped up again, this time in satisfaction. The earring they'd found in the bottom of the well was an exact match for the earrings in this set.

"Wow…" Penny exhaled a shaky breath. "Okay, so the earring in the well was stolen from the antique shop."

"Looks like," Stewart agreed.

"By Caleb?" Penny's gaze rose to meet his. "He was local, he knew a lot of *Englishers* in town, was friendly and well-known, would have known the store, most likely..."

"That's not proof, though," he countered. "That's entirely circumstantial. It would never stand up in court."

"I agree, but you have to admit it's a strong possibility," she replied.

Stewart's mind spun forward, arranging his victim and the assailant on the murder scene. Why would someone kill him?

"If he was the robber, could he have been killed trying to sell the jewelry?" Stewart asked. "Maybe someone was meeting him there. Maybe it was a sale gone wrong— someone lashing out, hitting him, grabbing the jewelry and then tossing his body down the well. Maybe in the rush, the earring snagged on his clothing and went down with him."

Stewart could see it coming together. A scuffle, a struggle, both men trying to stay quiet so as not to attract attention... But wasn't there a car that people mentioned— someone who took him away in a vehicle?

"All on the very night that the Amish community pulled together to help him…" Penny murmured.

"Who was the owner of the antique store?" Stewart asked.

Penny flipped through some pages. "Aaron Gelesky. At the time he was thirty-two."

"He'd be about eighty now, then," Stewart said. "Let's see if we can track him down. Maybe he can explain why an antique store would have had such an expensive set of jewelry to begin with."

Stew met her gaze again, and Penny shrugged faintly. He could throw himself into this case, and he knew Penny could bury herself in it with even more ease. But they'd shared a kiss a few minutes ago, and Stewart didn't want to just pretend it hadn't happened.

"Pen…" he said softly.

"No," she said, shaking her head. "You want to talk about…it."

"That kiss," he clarified. Call it what it

was—they'd shared a kiss, and she'd kissed him back, too. That had been mutual.

"I said no!" Penny shook her head. "I know you rather well, Stew. You'll regret this. You're kind to say I'm cautious for a reason, but the truth is, I'm scarred. I don't know who I trust. I don't know what I want. And you deserve better than that. Okay? Let's not ruin the best friendship I've ever had over this."

Friendship. That's where she wanted it to stay. He swallowed. Yeah…that kiss had been miles over the line. He should just be grateful she was willing to forget it instead of handing him over to HR.

"Okay," Stewart said, but he felt a lump of emotion rising in his throat, all the same. "Let's find Aaron Gelesky."

NINE

Penny stood in her apartment that evening, staring into her fish tank with an overflowing heart.

That kiss had shaken her—mostly because when Stewart had kissed her, she'd felt her heart opening up to him in spite of herself, and that had been downright terrifying. It wasn't right to fall for a man without having chosen it. Her brain had to rule here, and it had not been in control during that kiss. Her brain told her to hang on to what she had, which was a great partner and friend, and not to risk losing that relationship in pursuit of something more.

Her phone rang, and she looked down to see her mother's number. She picked up the call and headed over to the kitchen where her kettle had started to boil.

"Hi, Mom," she said. "How are you holding up?"

For the first few minutes, they talked about what *Mammi* was going through with all this new information coming at her. *Mammi* had gone to bed, and everything had been calm and peaceful. Yes, Sarah had seen the patrol cars. No, there hadn't been any sign of a problem.

"But what about you, Mom?" Penny asked. "How are you feeling about all of this?"

"I'm…feeling betrayed all over again," Sarah admitted softly. "I'd made my peace with one version of my father, only to get more questions. Was he a thief? Was he helping someone hide stolen goods? Who was he?"

"A liar, it would seem," Penny said softly.

"And I knew that," Sarah said. "It just hurts every time it is confirmed again. I haven't forgiven my father for walking out on us. I don't think I ever will."

"We'd better try," Penny said. "Carrying around that anger will only hurt us, not him. He's dead."

Her mother sighed. "Very wise, my dear. So why do you sound so miserable? Is this about your grandfather?"

"It's about my partner," she said.

"What about him?" Sarah asked. "Is everything all right?"

"I kissed him." She hadn't meant to blurt it out quite like that, but it was what it all boiled down to, wasn't it? Stewart might have started that kiss, but she'd certainly finished it! She'd kissed her longtime work partner, and now Stewart was being cautious with her, and distant. Of course he was! She couldn't blame him for that—after a kiss like theirs, things would be awkward.

"Well now…" Her mother was silent for a few beats. "I say about time. He'd handsome, sweet, and quite frankly, better than any other man you've been seeing lately."

"You've got to be kidding!" Penny retorted. "He's my colleague, my work partner! I can't go changing that relationship. Let's say something starts up between us."

"Okay?" Her mother sounded irritatingly cheery.

"And what if he ended up like the rest, Mom," Penny said softly.

"Disappointing you," Sarah murmured.

"Breaking my heart," Penny said bluntly. "When I get my heart broken, Stewart's the solid one who tells me I need to aim higher. I need that from him. I need him to remind me of those things, and if I mess things up with him…"

If she let herself feel too much and Stewart broke her heart, it would be like a mountain crumbling under her feet. What they had was perfect for her, and changing it would only open her up to more disappointment than she could bear. She had enough men letting her down in her life, and she needed one of them to remain his noble, stable self. Just one...

"If he broke your heart, then you'd lean on me," her mother said softly. "You do have a mother, you know."

"I don't want to play with this friendship," Penny said. She didn't want to let herself feel that dizzying, soft, melting feeling of slipping into his arms again. Because that feeling was not strength, it was letting go...it was falling...

"Then, don't do it," her mother replied. "You're smart, Penny. I trust your gut."

Penny would put it behind her. That was what she'd do. So after she'd finished chatting with her mother, she crawled into bed with her Bible and opened it to read a little bit before she went to sleep.

Her Bible fell open to an underlined passage that often brought her comfort in the book of Psalms.

Nevertheless I am continually with thee: thou hast holden me by my right hand. Thou shalt guide me with thy counsel, and afterward receive me to glory.

God had been her comfort all these years, through different boyfriends, through various heartbreaks, through the knowledge that the men in her family line hadn't been worthy of a woman's steadfast love. God had been there, and she'd always clung to that passage that promised God would guide her with His counsel. Because a word from God would go a long way right now!

I kissed Stewart, Lord, she prayed silently. *I don't think I should have done that...*

It wasn't a confession, exactly, but she was opening up her heart to her Maker. Her family line was filled with scarred, hurt women, and they all needed healing. People said healing took time, but for them it seemed to be taking generations...

She closed her Bible and turned off the

lamp. Maybe things would look less complicated in daylight.

The next morning, Stewart came by her place in the cruiser and texted her when he was outside her building. She headed down and when she got into the car, Stewart silently handed her a large paper cup of coffee.

"Thanks," she said, and she cracked open the lid and took a sip. It was perfect—double double, just the way she liked it. She stole a look at him out of the corner of her eye, and he cut her some side-eye at the same time.

"Are we okay?" Stewart asked.

"Yes, absolutely."

"Good." And his grip on the steering wheel loosened. "I'm glad. I was kind of worried last night."

"Don't be," she said. "We're good enough friends to handle a little, unexpected kiss."

"Of course we are," he said, nodding a couple of times. "We know each other better than anyone at this point, and I think it's just that we crossed lines into personal space. We met each other's parents, and..."

"It can feel confusing," she agreed. "That's the sort of relationship step that normally happens romantically."

"But I mean, with friends, too, right?" he asked.

"Yes, yes, of course."

They were both being a little too positive and earnest here, but it was the start of putting that far-too-memorable kiss behind them. She reached over and took his hand, giving it a squeeze. A friendly squeeze.

Stewart squeezed back and he shot her a warm smile. Her stomach tumbled, and she took a sip of coffee to distract herself.

He was a handsome man, a truly good man, too...but he was her friend. And she wouldn't be forgetting that again. Maybe she still needed a little comfort, and Stewart had always been just that to her—a powerful comfort when the world tipped upside down. She let go of his hand.

This morning, they were headed to see Aaron Gelesky, the owner of the robbed antique shop in Little Dusseldorf. They needed answers about that earring.

The address they were looking for turned out to be a squat little bungalow on a nice-sized corner lot. It was painted a cheery yellow, and an old man knelt on a cushion, pulling weeds in a front yard flower garden.

Penny and Stewart both got out, and they headed up the walk. The old man turned and pushed himself slowly and carefully to his feet.

"Hello," he said. "What can I do for you?"

"We're looking for Aaron Gelesky," Penny said.

"You're speaking to him," the old man said.

"We're from the Pennsylvania State Police," Stewart said, "and we're looking into an old case. We came across a robbery that happened years ago at your antique shop, and we thought it might be connected to our current case."

"What are you investigating?" Aaron asked.

"We'd rather not say right now," Penny said. "Do you mind if we ask you a few questions?"

"Suit yourself," the old man said. "You might as well come inside. I'll get you something to drink, if you like."

He led the way into the house. It was tidy, and a small, elderly dog got up from a cushion and started to bark hoarsely in their direction. They passed through the living room and into the kitchen. The old man pulled out two cans of cola from the fridge and waggled them in their direction.

"Thank you, that looks good," Penny said with a friendly smile.

They each took a can of pop, and then a seat at the table. The old man sat opposite them, eyeing them curiously.

"I don't get too many visitors these

days," he said. "Forgive me for enjoying this a bit."

"Can you tell us about that robbery?" Stewart asked.

"I had an antique shop in Little Dusseldorf, as you know," Aaron said. "And it was doing pretty well, too. Tourists like antiques and anything connected with the Amish. Even back then—it was all very novel. Anyway, one day we found the wires to the security camera had been cut, the door smashed, and one very valuable set of jewelry had been taken."

"That was it?" Penny asked. "Nothing else?"

It was possible that something hadn't been reported.

"Nothing. Not even a pen." The old man shook his head slowly. "Whoever came in knew what they were going for. And there's many people who knew about that necklace-and-earring set."

"Where did you get it from?" Penny asked.

"There was an estate sale for an old woman who'd been quite a hoarder," Aaron replied. "Her family didn't want to deal with the mess, and they were selling the contents of a house for a rather reasonable amount. The only hitch was we had to go through it all ourselves and fill dumpsters with the garbage. It was a huge amount of work, but there were quite a few novelties in the house, too."

"Including the jewelry?" Stewart asked.

"Yep. It was in the bottom of a trunk that had an antique wedding dress and some old books in there, too. I spent $500 for everything in that house, and I made back thousands."

"And the jewelry?" Stewart pressed.

"The jewelry…" The old man leaned back in his chair. "I had it appraised and it was worth thousands, and that was fifty years ago. I wasn't going to leave it in the shop for long—it certainly wasn't on display. I had it tucked up inside the closet in the office."

"And whoever stole it knew where to look," Stewart said. "Do you have any ideas on who that could be?"

"The only ones were my wife and kids. Thankfully, the jewelry was insured with the rest of our contents, and I got the insurance money for the whole set."

"The family—were they angry that you'd kept that jewelry?" Stewart asked.

"There was only a nephew, and he'd left the US before I even bought the contents. That was being taken care of by a lawyer. There was no one on American soil to even care. I don't think he ever knew about the jewelry."

"Do you remember his name?" Penny asked.

The old man shook his head.

"Was there anyone in town—friends, family, anyone at all—who knew about that jewelry?" Penny pressed.

"I'm sorry to say that a lot of people did," Aaron said. "I didn't mean to have word spread, exactly, but word got out. I'd talked to my family about it, and my daughter told a friend at school, and my son was working some odd hours at an Amish shop in Little Dusseldorf, and…well, before I knew it, everyone seemed to have heard about it. But not everyone knew where it was kept. I was looking for a buyer—I didn't want to hold on to something that pricey."

"Do you remember Caleb Renno?" Penny asked.

"Caleb Renno… Yeah, yeah, I remember him. An Amish fellow, right?" His face brightened. "I liked Caleb. He was a nice guy, or at least he seemed nice. I'm not condoning him running off and leaving his family like he did."

"Did you ever think he might have stolen the jewelry?" Stewart asked.

Aaron shook his head. "Well, I suppose it's a possibility, considering his character turned out to be much different than I thought. I *thought* he was a loyal family man. But I have to tell you, he wasn't the dishonest type. He'd find a dime on the floor and give it back to you. He was that kind of guy."

"Do you remember who he spent time with?" Penny asked. "I know it was a long time ago, but it would help us a lot."

"The only guy I remember was the owner of the hotel, Mike Miller. Mike and I were good friends, but Mike and Caleb were very close—it was strange. Amish and *English* don't tend to be that tight, but those two were very close pals."

Yes, and they knew why Caleb didn't share that standoffish attitude toward the *Englishers* now.

"Are you looking into Caleb's disappearance?" Aaron asked, leaning forward.

Penny and Stewart didn't answer, but they exchanged a look.

"Because I can tell you something about that," Aaron went on. "Caleb was a proud man, and he was doing some furniture delivery for me to make some extra money while he was out of work. That was after the robbery. And he was talking to me about his wife. He loved her. I mean, he really loved her. He said she was the best thing that ever happened to him, and he was determined to get another good job to provide for his family. I just… I can't imagine him just walking out on them. It didn't make sense."

They talked with him a little bit longer, asked more questions, but couldn't find out anything more than they already knew. When they'd exhausted every avenue, Stewart gave Penny a questioning look, and she shrugged. They were done here.

"Thank you for your time, Aaron," Stewart said, shaking the old man's hand. "We appreciate it."

When they got back into the car, Stewart said, "He had no intention of leaving his family."

"But he may very well have stolen the jewelry," she said.

"But why hold on to it for a year when

he was in such a financial crunch?" Stewart asked.

"Maybe he didn't know how to unload it. I mean, he was a simple man living an Amish life. Who would he sell an expensive necklace and set of earrings to?"

Stewart met her gaze, and for a moment they were both silent.

"He might not have done it, Penny," he said quietly.

"You're trying to make me feel better," she said. "Don't do that. We need the truth, not a comfortable lie."

"I'm looking for the truth, too," Stewart said. "But it's not always ugly."

No, it wasn't always ugly, but in their line of work, it tended to be. And she didn't need false hope that would only be dashed later. In her experience, the truth of the matter was normally more painful than the comfortable veneer everyone had accepted as the truth.

A wise woman was a careful woman, and that was the truest thing she knew.

* * *

Once they were settled in the car again, Stewart's mind flipped through their leads.

"Where to now?" Penny asked.

"Let's go down to the Shady Oaks Retirement Lodge and find Mike Miller," Stewart said. "He keeps coming up again and again, doesn't he? I think it's high time we had a chat with him."

"That's a good idea," Penny agreed, and she fastened her seat belt. "We should sit down with Robert Fuller, too. He was another one of Caleb's *Englisher* friends, and he's at the same retirement home."

"We'll get to the bottom of this," he said.

"That's what I'm afraid of," she murmured.

Stewart pulled away from the curb and headed back toward the highway. He could tell that Penny was bracing herself for the worst with this case. They saw victim's families doing this all the time—refusing to get their hopes up because every time they did it hurt so much worse when they were disappointed. He always felt bad for people when they were going through such tough times, but watching Penny do the same thing slipped under his armor. It made him want to tear everything apart just to get her the answers she needed.

While Stewart drove, Penny pored over the case from her phone. She had photos of the crime scene, of the body, of the evidence…and he wished she'd take a break from it all, but he knew better than to say anything. Penny got results because she immersed herself in her cases. This was her strength as a cop.

The Shady Oaks Retirement Lodge on the west end of Little Dusseldorf was an attractive building with a rather pinched and small parking lot. Stewart found a spot, and he and Penny headed into the building through the front doors.

Several residents were shuffling through the foyer, and a nurse was directing them down another hall where there was a sign that read Social Mixer—Let's Dance!

Stewart went over to the front desk and showed the receptionist his badge.

"We're looking for two gentlemen who live here. One is named Robert Fuller and the other is Mike Miller," Stewart said.

"Yes, they're both here. Is there a problem, Detective?"

"No, no, there's no emergency," he replied. "We just wanted to ask them about some people they may have known years ago, pertaining to another case."

"Did you need to talk to them together, or—"

"Individually is best," he replied. "Maybe we can start with Robert Fuller."

The young woman's eyes sparkled with curiosity, but she picked up the phone and murmured into it. A woman in nursing scrubs approached and gave them a smile.

"I can bring you to Mr. Fuller," she said. "He's already at the dance. He can really shake a tail feather."

"Oh yeah?" Stewart couldn't help but chuckle. "Thanks. We appreciate it."

They followed the nurse down the hall-way toward the room. The lights were low, the room was decorated with balloons, and some music from the fifties was crooning from speakers in a corner. An old fellow with a walker was standing with another old woman swaying to the music.

"That's Robbie," the nurse said. "Let me go let him know you're here."

The old man looked over his shoulder when the nurse spoke to him and he eyed them curiously. He gave the old woman a gallant nod and tip of an imaginary hat and then hoisted up his walker to follow the nurse in their direction. He had a round face, albeit lined now, and what was left of his hair was white.

"We're sorry to interrupt a good time," Stewart said. "But we need to ask you a few questions. Do you mind?"

"Mind? I never turn down a visitor," Robbie replied. "Lead the way."

The nurse indicated an office that was empty, and Penny went in first. There was a desk with a few chairs inside. Robbie took a seat and looked up at them expectantly.

"Do you remember Caleb Renno?" Stewart asked.

"Sure do." Robbie sobered. "He was a real piece of work, that guy."

"How so?" Penny asked.

"He left his family, didn't he? His wife was a sweet woman, too. She loved him, and he had great kids. The Amish believe in family—that's what makes them different. They don't get divorced—ever! It's against their rules. And then Caleb up and left her."

"Do you remember a robbery in the area?" Penny asked. "It was an antiques store."

"Yeah, I do…" Robbie nodded. "Some expensive jewelry was stolen. I tried to track that jewelry down for years. I figured it should have popped up eventually once everything calmed down, but it never did."

"Did you have any suspects?" Stewart asked.

"A few."

"Was Caleb on that list?" Penny asked.

"He might have been." Robbie shook his head. "He didn't strike me as the type of guy who'd know how to unload a bunch of cut gems if he dismantled the jewelry, or just some expensive jewelry, period. I knew him. He was a simple guy. Amish men don't fit the MO for that kind of robbery."

Robbie didn't know Caleb that well, apparently.

"Did you ever hear from him again?" Penny asked.

"Nope. When he was gone, he was gone."

"Did you suspect he might have been killed?" Stewart asked.

"Killed? You'd need a body for that. No, I think he just left. He wasn't as decent as we thought."

"Did you keep in contact with his widow?" Penny asked.

Robbie shook his head. "She was still married in her mind. And even if she weren't, I'm not Amish. There are lines."

Stewart exchanged a look with Penny.

"Well, thank you for your time, Robbie. Enjoy the dance."

"Will do." Robbie pushed himself to his feet, and Penny pulled the door open for him to let him head back the festivities. The old woman was waiting for him at the door and she fluttered her fingers at him.

Stewart smothered a smile, and turned toward the nurse who approached.

"Can I talk with Mike Miller, please?" Stewart asked.

"Sure. Mr. Miller is in the library."

Stewart and Penny followed the nurse down a hallway, the music from the dance fading away as they headed up a flight of stairs and down another hallway, emerging into a large, pleasant, book-lined room. There were couches, tables, a large electric fireplace and some spacious windows letting in a quantity of daylight. A lot of effort had been put into transforming what had probably been a meeting room into a cozy, comforting library. A plaque on the wall stated that the room had been funded by several businesses in town.

An old man sat by a window, a book open in his lap and a magnifying glass in one hand to help him read. He had sparse, wispy white hair on his head, and he wore dress pants, a nice quality sweater, and a pair of leather slippers on his feet.

"Mr. Miller," the nurse said, approaching the man and bending down. "There are some police officers who want to talk with you. Is that okay?"

The old man looked around hesitantly. "Oh, yes. I suppose so. Police, you say?"

The nurse stepped back, and Penny took the lead this time. She pulled up a chair in front of the old man and gave him a friendly smile.

"Are you Michael Miller?" she asked. "The same who used to own Slumber Inn in town?"

"That's me, all right," the old man said. "Call me Mike."

"My name is Detective Penny Moore, and this is my partner, Detective Stewart Jones," she said. "We just had a few questions for you, if you have the time."

"I've got nothing but time these days," Mike said. "Should I have someone here with me for this talk?"

"Are you asking if you need a lawyer?" Stewart asked.

"I don't have a lawyer. Who walks around with a lawyer on retainer? Not the likes of me. I owned a motel—and not anything fancy! I was thinking of my son," Mike replied.

"We just have a few questions about a man you would have known but your son wouldn't have met," Penny said. "But it's up to you."

"I guess it's all right." Mike pushed his book aside.

"You weren't interested in the dance down there?" Stewart asked, attempting to help the old man relax. It seemed to work, because Mike smiled ruefully.

"I'm not much of a dancer. I step on toes. How can I help?"

"We are looking into the disappearance of Caleb Renno," Penny said. "He vanished forty-eight years ago."

"And his body was recovered, I was told," Mike said quietly.

So Mike had been keeping up with local news, it seemed. He was more in the know than Robbie had been downstairs. The old man's eyes clouded, and he dropped his gaze.

"Yes, it was," Penny confirmed. "Do you know Robert Fuller? He lives here in the lodge, too."

"Of course. Everyone knows everyone."

"He didn't know that Caleb was dead," Stewart said. "But you do."

"We aren't close pals or anything," Mike said. "We don't talk about that."

"An old friend who disappeared and whose body was found?" Penny shook her head. "That seems like something in common to discuss. Not terribly personal."

"We didn't talk about it. Robbie's a bit of a womanizer, if you didn't know. He tries to sweet-talk every woman in this place, including the nurses. I have more respect for women than that. I don't like him. So we don't talk."

Stewart and Penny exchanged a look.

"Well, we just wanted to know a bit more about Caleb Renno. We understand that you were particularly good friends with him."

"A very long time ago, he was my best friend," Mike said.

"Did you believe he'd left his family?" Stewart asked.

Mike blinked up at him, looking momentarily confused. "Um, yes. Yes, I did. Like everyone else, I thought he'd left them."

"Did that seem like something he would do?" Penny asked.

"Well…he seemed to have done it, and we all just got used to that," Mike replied.

"And like any man, he'd complained about his wife from time to time. He told me once that he'd considered leaving, so this wasn't out of the blue, exactly. He could have done it. It had crossed his mind, and you never know what goes on behind closed doors, do you?"

"Was there another woman?" Penny asked.

"No, not Caleb. He was many things, but he wasn't a cheater," Mike replied.

"Knowing that he was killed, though," Stewart said, "do you have any idea who might have done it?"

"Killed him?" Mike's lips trembled. "No. No. Who would do that? No."

They were upsetting him—that was clear, and Stewart pulled up another chair to get down to the old man's level, a non-verbal way of lowering the stress. They didn't need to intimidate him. They needed him comfortable.

"What did he complain about in his marriage?" Penny asked.

It was a good question, but the answer might hurt for Penny. She sat very still, picking at her thumbnail in her lap.

"Oh… Elizabeth didn't give him enough attention when she was focused on the children." Mike shrugged. "Elizabeth told her sisters too much about their relationship… That sort of thing. Sometimes they'd fight and he'd be so angry that he just wanted to walk away. For good, if you know what I mean."

"But those reasons don't seem like something that would drive a man away permanently," Stewart said.

"There were other things, too," Mike said defensively. "I just don't recall. This was a very long time ago."

"That's fair," Penny said quietly.

"Caleb's wife is a good woman," Mike added. "She raised those kids on her own after Caleb…died—we can say that now, can't we? Well, she raised them alone, and she worked hard to keep them fed and to keep them in school clothes, and... She was a good woman."

"Did you stay connected to her?" Penny asked.

"Of course, I did," Mike replied. "I did everything I could for her. I brought her groceries, I gave her money when I was able to scrape it up, and I'd get her things she needed like more cloth to make clothes for her kids or supplies for her home."

"That was generous of you," Penny said.

"He was my friend," Mike said. "And I cared. It was too bad she couldn't have remarried. If she'd been another faith, she would have been permitted. She could have claimed abandonment and gotten another husband. But the Amish aren't like that. Marriage is for life, and if her husband was still alive, she couldn't marry until he, well, until he wasn't alive anymore."

"So you helped her live more comfortably," Stewart said.

"As much as she'd let me," he replied. "I'm not Amish, so..."

"And how did your wife feel about that?" Penny asked.

"She didn't like it," Mike said. "But she knew it wasn't for romantic reasons. I was just trying to do right by my friend's wife. But she didn't like that I cared as much as I did, I'll admit that."

"Did you become friends with Elizabeth?" Stewart asked.

"Of sorts. She'd tell me when she really needed something," he replied. "She vented on me a few times, too. She did some yelling and crying and… Well, I suppose she needed to let it all out. If you'd call that friendship, then I suppose I'm her friend."

"Do you see her still?" Penny asked.

"I'm cooped up here now," he replied. "Sometimes my granddaughter will take me out for lunch, or my son will come by and we'll play chess together. But it's not so easy to get out and see Elizabeth as it used to be."

There was a certain tenderness in the old man's voice when he said Elizabeth's name, and Stewart had to wonder if Mike had been in love with his friend's wife. There seemed to be a pretty close connection there.

"What happened to your wife?" Stewart asked.

"She died twenty years ago of breast cancer," he replied.

"I'm sorry to hear that," Penny said.

"Thanks." Mike sighed. "So…do you have any idea who…who…you know…killed him?"

It was hard for Mike to even say it, but Stewart shook his head.

"Not yet," he replied. "We're doing our best."

"Oh, one more question, Mike," Penny said. "On the night that Caleb disappeared—or was killed—many people said they heard that Caleb had left in a car with someone."

"Did they say that?" Mike murmured.

"Did you see him leave?" Penny asked.

Mike shook his head. "No, I didn't see

him at all. I arrived too late. I got there when Elizabeth was crying."

Stewart looked over at Penny, and she pressed her lips together in the way that said she was done with all the questions she had. He gave her a slight nod in return.

"Thank you for your time, Mike," Penny said, shaking the old man's hand. "We appreciate it."

Stewart stood up and waited for Penny to rise, too. Stewart let Penny go ahead of him, and they headed back down the hallway, down the stairs and toward the door with a Loretta Lynn song wailing in from the dance.

When they were back in the car again, Stewart exhaled a slow breath.

"So what did we learn?" Penny asked, pulling out her phone to take notes.

"Robert Fuller first," Stewart said. "He had some suspicions, but the jewelry never surfaced again. At least, not that he could find. And yet another person to say he didn't believe Caleb could leave his family."

"Mike Miller sure did, though," she replied. "Was he just a closer friend?"

"He said Caleb talked about leaving. But Caleb didn't leave. He was murdered..." Stewart sighed.

"He didn't hear the rumor about Caleb leaving in a car," Penny said, typing into her phone. "He's the only one who didn't hear that rumor."

"Also, I can't prove it, but I have a feeling Mike Miller was in love with your grandmother," Stewart added.

Penny looked up then and met his gaze. "He was helping."

"Trust me, Pen," he said, his voice low. "He was in love with her. A man doesn't notice every little thing a woman needs and provide it for her out of Christian charity. It was deeper than that. Maybe not for her, but for him, it was."

"You bring me coffee all the time," she said with a low laugh.

And that hit him like a punch in the chest. Yeah, he did. And he noticed her moods, and knew when she needed distraction. He knew when she was hurting, and he knew her favorite treats, and her ways to bust stress...

A man didn't do all of that because he was her partner. He did it because she'd slipped into his heart somewhere along the way, and he couldn't help himself.

He cleared his throat and started the car.

"Let's get back to the station," he said gruffly. He wasn't ready to face that just yet.

TEN

Penny ran her fingers through her hair and flicked through the pictures of evidence as they headed back toward the station. Nothing was new, of course, but she was waiting for the pieces to slide together in her mind and give her a clear picture of what happened. This was how it worked.

They'd looked into Willard's past in Pittsburgh, but they hadn't turned up anything useful. But something that Mike Miller had said was tugging at her brain. He'd said he helped out the family a lot after Caleb disappeared. He'd come by and brought items they needed… He'd obviously been very friendly with Elizabeth, and possibly in love with her.

But Elizabeth *had let* him. That was the

surprising part. She had an Amish community to help her get back on her feet and help support her. So why allow an *Englisher* man in, that close to her home? It didn't make sense.

Unless he'd been lying about that?

"Do you think Mike was telling the truth?" Penny asked after a few minutes of silence.

"Hmm?" Stewart looked over at her.

"Mike—was he lying?" she asked.

Stewart pursed his lips in thought, his gaze back on the road again. "Maybe. It's hard to tell. But lying about what?"

"About being as close to the family as he claimed. He said he helped a lot—brought them things. Was that true?"

"Do you think he might have wanted to help and just made it up?"

"Maybe he wanted to look more heroic than he was," she said.

"How do we check up on it?"

Asking *Mammi* directly might not be the way to get to the truth. Having an *Eng-*

lisher man providing help might look quite bad to her community, and she might be tempted to cover that up. *Mammi* wouldn't lie, exactly, but she might evade the truth. No, if they wanted to check up on Mike's story, they'd need to ask someone else. At least at first.

"My mother might remember," Penny said. "She was twelve when *Dawdie* disappeared, so Mike's presence in their home would have been in her early teenaged years. She'd have been old enough to remember that pretty clearly."

"True. Why don't you give her a call?" Stewart said.

Penny was already swiping through her contacts, and she tapped her mother's number and put her earbuds into her ears. It rang once and Sarah picked up.

"Hi, Penny," she said. "How's the investigation going?"

"It's…going," Penny said. "Look, I wanted to ask you about someone who's claiming to have been pretty close to your family when you were growing up."

"Who?" Sarah asked.

"Mike Miller, *Dawdie*'s good *Englisher* friend. Do you remember him at all?"

"I do remember him. He used to come by for supper sometimes before my father left—before he died, I should say," Sarah said. "And he came by from time to time after he left, too."

"How often?"

"I don't recall exactly. Regularly, though. He would bring boxes of groceries and stuff like that. My mother was always grateful—we were pretty broke with my dad gone."

"What sort of relationship did he have with your mother?" Penny asked.

"I don't know. They chatted. He was… compassionate. I remember my mother crying sometimes—missing my father, feeling betrayed—and Mike would help her to feel better. He'd bring her new cloth to make us some clothes, or he'd come with a store-bought cake sometimes—the kind with icing flowers on top. We loved that."

"So he was a part of things," Penny said.

"Yeah, I guess he was. My mom needed support."

"He was married, of course," Penny said.

"Oh, I don't think it was romantic. He'd always been friendly with my mother—even before my dad disappeared."

He'd been around. He'd been part of things. He'd been an emotional support to *Mammi* after *Dawdie* disappeared. He'd been rather heroic from a woman's perspective. But why would he do all of that with his own wife and kids at home? Why would he step in and be the man in another home?

"So they were good friends?" Penny asked cautiously.

"He was a really nice man," Sarah said. "He was kind to us. And he was kind to my mother. He used to tell her that she was beautiful, and ask us kids if we agreed.

And she'd blush and get all embarrassed. But he made her smile again."

"Like a boyfriend?" Penny asked.

"No!" Sarah said, then she paused. "At the time, I didn't even question that. I was a kid. I knew that my mother couldn't re-marry because my father was out there somewhere, living it up as *Englisher*—or so we imagined."

"As an adult looking back on it?" Penny pressed. "Did they seem…infatuated with each other, maybe?"

"Maybe," Sarah admitted. "My mother cared about him. She used to brighten up when his car pulled into the drive. Maybe she'd developed some feelings for him. And I don't blame her. She was alone."

But was it possible that those tender feelings had developed before Caleb vanished? That was the question swimming through Penny's mind. She wouldn't dare suggest it to her mother, though. Sarah would defend her own mother's reputation to her dying breath. In fact, it was Penny's instinct, too.

But what if Caleb's good friend Mike had wormed his way into Elizabeth's heart while her husband still lived? What if their marital discord had been about Mike? Uncle Isaac had mentioned some jealousy about another man. What if Caleb wanted to move his family away from that community to get his wife away from his *Englisher* best friend? That might explain the passionate arguments.

Penny's heart pounded in her throat. This was moving in a very ugly direction.

"Okay, well, that's helpful. I was just wondering if Mike was lying about it. Thanks, Mom," Penny said, trying to sound casual.

"Are you on to something?" Sarah pressed.

"I don't know," Penny said. "I'll keep you posted. But I'd better get going."

She said her farewells and ended the call. Stewart cast her a quick, pointed look.

"What are you thinking?" Stewart asked.

"I hate to admit what I'm thinking," she breathed.

"Lay it out. It's just an idea, nothing proven," Stewart said. "Lay it out for me, and we can pick it apart."

"Can I trust you not to tell anyone about this theory just yet?" Penny asked.

"Of course. I'm serious, Pen. This is your family. I'm being really careful. I'm not reporting anything until we're certain."

She exhaled a shaky breath. "I'm wondering if Elizabeth and Mike might have developed a rather close relationship before Caleb disappeared. We know Elizabeth and Caleb were fighting a lot—the family all mentioned it. And Caleb wanted to move the family to a different community. Elizabeth didn't want to go. But what if Caleb's reason for wanting to move them was because he saw something developing between his wife and his *Englisher* best friend? What if their last big fight was about Mike?"

"Go on…"

"What if Elizabeth went away from the house into the woods to fight with her husband out of earshot of the kids, and in a moment of rage she picked up a piece of wood and swung it—"

"What if Elizabeth killed her husband after all," Stewart breathed.

"That's what I'm wondering," Penny admitted. "It would make sense, wouldn't it? It would make the pieces all come together."

"But like you said, she'd need help to get the body into the well."

"Maybe Mike helped her. He stuck around in her life afterward. He was a part of her life, he was helpful, and like you said, he seemed to be in love with her. I hate that I'm saying this, but maybe he helped cover up a murder."

"She went the last forty-eight years believing he'd disappeared, though," Stewart said. "You saw her reaction when we told her that he was dead. She was truly shocked."

"You're right." Relief flooded through her. "You're right…"

"I've seen a lot of guilty people, Pen," Stewart said. "And your grandmother seemed legitimately shocked at the news that Caleb was dead and on the property all this time. And in her sometimes confused state of mind, I don't think she could fake that."

"So, maybe it was innocent after all…just a friend of the family who cared enough to help."

"It's possible for a guy to develop feelings and not have them returned," Stewart said quietly. "Mike could have been head over heels in love with his best friend's widow, and never acted on it. He was married, after all, and had a family of his own."

"Or those more romantic feelings may have developed after his wife's passing," Penny suggested.

"True. He said she died twenty years ago, right? So that's some time for him to start feeling more for Elizabeth."

"But as an Amish woman, she'd never look at him that way," Penny said. "The

Amish don't marry outsiders, and she believed her husband still lived."

It still didn't make sense, and while Stewart was giving her some good reasons to believe in her grandmother's innocence, it was the best explanation so far, and she hated that.

They arrived at the station, and Stewart parked and turned off the engine. Penny didn't reach for the door handle, though. Her mind was still spinning. She noticed a truck across the street from the station—a mud-covered pickup. But just as she spotted it, it eased away from the curb and disappeared around the corner.

"Penny—" Stewart reached out and caught her hand.

Her heartbeat hammered hard against her ribs, but it was just a truck. Muddied vehicles were pretty common around here with all the farms. Was she getting paranoid?

Stewart's warm, strong grip was so reassuring, as everything else around her seemed to be as stable as sand. She

looked up at him and found those chocolate brown eyes moving over her face. "Are
you okay?"

"I'm fine."

He didn't answer, but he didn't seem to
believe her, either. She should pull her hand
free, but looking over at her loyal partner,
she was tired of running.

"I'm not fine," she admitted softly. "I'm
jumpy with this cold case. Family lore has
a way of giving you a bedrock to build
your life on, and when you find out that the
lore wasn't exactly true, everything shifts."

"What's shifting right now?" Stewart
turned in his seat as much as he could to
angle his body toward her.

"Everything I trusted." Her belief in her
grandmother's pure heart, and her grandfather's vile character, for one. Her understanding of how their relationship had
worked, and the sort of man a woman
should avoid. Was Caleb a bad man, or
just a rightfully jealous husband? Would
he have left his family if he hadn't been

killed, or were people painting him in a worse light to defend their own actions?

"I'm not changing," Stewart said softly. "You can count on me. I'm the same stubborn, boring partner I've always been."

"You aren't boring," she said. "Far from that."

"Yeah?" He squeezed her hand. "But I am stable. I haven't changed, and I won't. I'm here for you."

She looked down at their hands, his broad palm covering hers protectively, and then she looked up into his eyes, so tender, so warm… He'd always been this way, she realized in a rush. He'd never asked anything of her. He'd never suggested more between them, but he'd always been this way. And she'd started to depend on him over the years more than she even should. It was possible for a man to develop feelings for a woman and never have them returned…wasn't that what he'd said?

"Stew," she whispered.

Stewart leaned closer, the seat creaking,

and her gaze dropped down to his lips. He seemed to have the same thought, because he reached up and touched her chin with the pad of his thumb. She lifted her lips, and his mouth came down over hers in a soft, gentle kiss that felt like the wild relief of spring rains after a long, hard winter. His kiss was so gentlemanly—no demands, just tenderness there for her taking if she wanted it...

And she realized that she did want this kiss more than anything, and she leaned into him. As she did, his kiss changed and became something more. He broke it off then, and when she opened her eyes, his were still shut.

"I said I wouldn't do that again," he breathed, and he opened his eyes. "But I've been wanting to kiss you for a really long time."

"I didn't know," she said. "You should have said something."

"Said something?" He laughed softly and shook his head. "I didn't even know what

I was feeling until recently. I couldn't put a name to it."

"What are you feeling?" Penny twined her fingers through his, and he squeezed gently. How did he define this strange, yearning between them, the stalwart friendship, the tender support?

"I fell in love with you," he said, his voice taut with emotion. "I'm sorry. I tried not to. I really did."

And her heart thundered to a stop.

Stewart shouldn't have said it. In fact, he was still a little stunned that he had, but it was true. Penny stared at him wide-eyed, and he wished he could take it back—rewind everything between them and start over. Would it change his feelings for her? Probably not, but there were times when a man's feelings didn't matter. There was right and there was wrong, and falling for his partner was definitely wrong.

"You…" Her breath just seemed to seep

out of her, and this was the first time he'd seen his partner speechless.

"Look, you can forget I said it," he suggested with a faint shrug.

"I don't think I can," she whispered.

He'd ruined everything, hadn't he? He looked down at their hands, fingers entwined, and she hadn't pulled back. He licked his lips.

"I didn't mean for this to happen," he said quietly. "I didn't even realize I was falling for you until recently. But I know you better than anyone, and you know me. I thought we were just a really well-matched pair of colleagues, but it's a whole lot more than that for me. I care about what you feel, about what you think, about whether or not you got a decent meal into you lately… I just…"

Penny looked at him mutely—why wasn't she helping him out here? He met her gaze helplessly.

"I just want to cook you dinner," he said at last.

That covered it, didn't it? He wanted to take care of her, make sure she was comfortable and happy. He wanted to listen to her, and get her advice. He wanted to make sure that she sat down at the end of a long day and had a good meal that would make her feel better. And on days when she needed it, he wanted to be the one who brought her donuts. He wanted to be her guy, he realized in a rush.

And he was in love with her.

"That sounds really wonderful," she said softly.

"Does it?" he asked hopefully.

"But it wouldn't last with us, Stew," she said, shaking her head. "I'm still going to be a workaholic. I'm still going to go overboard with my cases, pore over evidence when I'm supposed to be resting. I'm…just wired that way. And you're right, I do know you better than anyone, and I know what you need. You need a woman who will be a respite away from all of this. You aren't as tough as you look—and you look plenty tough. But this ugliness gets overwhelming for you, and as much as you push me to take a break, it's because it's what you need! I'm not good for you. I'll drive you crazy, and you'll end up doing what every other guy in our family does—"

"No!" he said firmly. "I'm not one of those guys, Penny."

"I'm also not what you need." Tears glistened in her eyes. "Every time you told me what you needed, I didn't check off those boxes. I think we're old enough to know that wishing and hoping doesn't change how a person is put together. You want someone who can provide comfort and some balance in your life."

She was right, of course. He did need a woman to stubbornly show him the beauty in the world, because sometimes he struggled to see it. This job took so much out of him that he had been utterly certain that he needed a woman outside of this demanding job. And then he went and fell in love with his partner.

"Whatever you're feeling for me—it won't last," Penny said.

"And it's one-sided," he concluded, a lump in his throat. He'd fallen for her, and she hadn't fallen for him. Story as old as time. Maybe it was better this way.

"What?" Penny shook her head. "You think I don't feel this, too?"

His heart hammered hard, then seemed to skip a beat.

"Do you?" he asked uncertainly.

"Yes!" Penny pulled her hand free of his grip then, and his palm suddenly felt cold. "Yes, I feel it. Stew, you're the perfect guy. I fell for you ages ago, but you're too perfect. You're kind, sweet, smart, focused... I know how this goes. We've fallen for each other, but sometimes people fall and it's not a good match...like my grandparents. Like my parents. Like...us."

Stewart's mind was spinning now. "So you feel this, too? Because I need to know if I am a complete and utter fool, or if this is just a tiny bit mutual."

In response, Penny leaned in and pressed her lips against his. Her kiss was filled with longing, and when she pulled back, a tear had slipped down her cheek.

"I love you, too, Stew," she whispered.

He slipped a hand behind her neck and tugged her in a little closer. He just wanted to hold her, to feel her pulse under his touch, to feel her breath against his face... Every instinct inside of him wanted to keep her close.

"But I can't take the risk," she whispered, and she pulled back. He let his hand drop. "You need a woman with balance and strength and a whole heart. I'm still working through issues, and all I see around me are women in my family loving hard and getting hurt. I can't do it. You're the closest friend I have in the world right now, and if anything went wrong between us, I'd lose more than a partner. I'd lose my best friend."

Penny was right about what they had to lose. If anything went wrong, he'd lose his best friend, too. Stewart exhaled a slow breath.

"So what do we do?" he asked.

"We work on the case," she said, and she swallowed hard. "We throw ourselves into the work. Finding answers helps people, and it helps distract us from things we don't want to think about, too."

For her, it did. This was how Penny dealt with almost everything—throwing herself into whatever case was in front of her. What he actually wanted to know was if they could go on being partners, sleuthing out clues, finding criminals and working together knowing how they both felt. Because Penny might be capable of just burying herself in the workload, but he wasn't.

"I actually need some time to myself without work in front of me," he said, his voice low.

"Oh… Okay," she said, and he could see the flicker of pain in her eyes. It had come out like a rejection.

"Look, I shouldn't have even told you

what I was feeling," he said. "I know it crossed a line, and it made things awkward for you. So I just need a bit of time to rein it all back in."

And looking at her—Penny appearing utterly vulnerable, her eyes misty and her cheeks pale—he wished there was some sort of solution for them. But she was right—they needed different things, and while falling for her hadn't been a choice, it hadn't been wise, either.

"Are you going to ask for a new partner?" Penny asked.

Maybe he would. He might have to if he couldn't get his own heart disentangled from hers. He wished he knew how successful this attempt would be, because right now he couldn't imagine stuffing all of these emotions back inside again.

"I just need a bit of time," he said, his throat tight. "If you want to keep working, I'll head home and—"

And what? He didn't even know. He'd head home and try to wrap his own head around this. How had he been so foolish? Why hadn't he kept his mouth shut? If he'd done that, he could have carried on working with Penny every day, but now? He might lose her for good anyway.

"I'm just going to head home," he concluded. "I'll see you in the morning."

Stewart could feel the weight of the unsaid words hanging between them, but they'd said enough. Anything more and they might go against all their instincts and end up back in each other's arms. It was better to stop things now before there was more pain.

Penny got out of the cruiser and she headed back toward the building. She looked back at him once, and the confused pain in her eyes made his stomach clench. He was the cause of this, and he truly had thought better of himself. He was supposed to be stronger. He'd carried the burden of his feelings for her for months—why crack now?

Stewart left the cruiser parked in their

spot, and when Penny disappeared into the building, he went over to where his black SUV waited and got in. He needed to get away from work, away from the case, away from other people's pain and find somewhere that he could think.

When he pulled out of the parking lot, he'd thought he was heading home, but then he took another turn and found himself driving in the direction of the old church he'd grown up in. It was a tall building with a steeple and siding that needed painting, but every time there was a work bee, people only managed to paint the first story, and the rest of it faded into disrepair. He was feeling a bit like that old church— falling apart faster than he could put himself back together again today.

Stewart pulled into the nearly empty parking lot. There were four vehicles scattered around it, and he parked nearby the front door. He sat for a couple of minutes with his hands on the steering wheel, wondering why he'd come.

People here couldn't understand the burdens he carried. They meant well, but their platitudes were no comfort to him. So why had he come?

"I wish I knew," he muttered to himself.

But he was here now, and he needed somewhere to just think and get his balance back again, and this church was as good a place as any, if he thought about it. At least he'd have a bit of privacy this evening, since it didn't look like anything was going on at the moment.

He sighed and got slowly out of his vehicle. He wasn't looking for human comfort or wisdom right now—he was looking for the kind of comfort that came from above.

The front door was propped open with a rock, and he headed inside. The church office was down a carpeted hallway off the far side of the foyer, and he could hear a woman on the phone answering some questions about Sunday's service. How many Sundays had he spent in this very building when he was growing up? There had been the regular services where he'd sat in the same row as his family, and then there were the youth evenings and work-bee Saturdays when he'd been one of the dutiful volunteers, slapping a coat of white paint as far as the first story. Back then, he'd thought he'd be able to find all of his answers within these walls. He'd thought that he'd marry a girl from this church, and raise his own kids here. But life hadn't turned out that way.

Stewart slipped past and through the swinging doors that led into the sanctuary. It was quiet and still, the smell of old wood varnish and dust tickling his nose. There was a faded bouquet at the front of the pulpit, flowers drooping, ready to be replaced. He sank into a back pew and rubbed his hands over his face.

O God, I think I messed things up, he prayed silently. *Really badly.*

He heard the squeak of floorboards, and he inwardly winced, then looked over his shoulder. The trim, elderly pastor came down the center aisle, then looked over at Stewart in surprise.

"Stew Jones," he said with a smile. "It's been a long while since I've seen you here."

"Hi, Pastor Bill," he said, and swallowed. "Sorry to disturb. I just came for some quiet."

"You came for some prayer," Pastor Bill said. "Say it like it is, Stew."

"I came for prayer," Stewart agreed.

The older man sat in the pew ahead of Stewart and looked toward the front of the sanctuary.

"I'm glad you're back," the pastor said, not turning.

"I'm not back, exactly," Stewart said.

"You're here, aren't you?" The older man looked over his shoulder at Stewart, then turned. "What brings you here today?"

"I don't really want to talk about it," Stewart said.

He nodded slowly. "You never did. Maybe that was the problem."

"Look, Pastor, I don't mean to offend, but

I don't think the things I see should be repeated," Stewart said. "That's my burden."

"Is that why you're here—something ugly at work?" the pastor asked.

"No," Stewart admitted. "I'm here because I've fallen in love with the wrong woman."

"Is she married?"

"No!"

"Is she a Christian?"

"Yes."

"Then I don't see a problem." A smile touched the old man's lips, and Stewart smiled back bitterly. If only things were so simple.

"It's complicated, Pastor."

"It always is, Stewart." The older man pressed his lips together. "Can I pray for you?"

"I don't know..."

"It's why you're here," the pastor said. "You can pray for yourself—and I encourage that. Pour out your heart to your Maker. But there seems to be a special answer that God reserves for when we pray for each other. I don't need to know details, Stew. Can I pray for you?"

"I suppose."

And Pastor Bill bowed his head and his rich voice seemed to spread out and fill the whole sanctuary with a sweet, low sound. He prayed for Stewart's job, for the burdens he carried. He prayed for Stewart's family, for his hopes for the future, for guidance. And he prayed for Stewart's future wife, who Pastor Bill was certain was out there. Whether she was the woman he loved presently, or he hadn't met her yet, the older man prayed that God would bless her, protect her, provide for her, and in His timing, bring them together. When he said Amen and opened his eyes, Stewart felt tears rising in his own.

"You don't have to do this alone," Pastor Bill said quietly, putting a warm hand on Stewart's shoulder. "Come back to church on Sunday. Give it another chance."

And Stewart found himself wondering

if he should. Maybe he didn't need to be fully understood. Maybe he just needed some prayers from people who didn't understand but who cared all the same. Because on his own, he didn't seem to have the answers, either.

And when he got back to his SUV, he found the driver's side window smashed, a deep, keyed scratch down one side and the word *pig* scratched into the driver's side door. A hunk of mud slapped in the center of his windshield. Written in mud across the hood were the words "stop it."

He scanned the nearly empty parking lot, looking up and down the quiet street. There was no one. But Stewart did have a dashboard cam. He opened up his vehicle and pulled down the camera and attached it to his phone. The last bit of motion it detected was a youngish-looking male with a black hoodie and a bandana pulled up over his face, then that slap of mud that obliterated his view. It wasn't much to go on... but this was a pretty young guy to have a personal interest in an almost fifty-year-old murder!

Whoever was doing this wanted to warn them away from the case. He flipped over to his phone camera to take pictures for evidence, and called the station. Maybe he'd get that distraction after all.

ELEVEN

Penny sat at her desk, an array of photos spread over the surface, a rattling box of thumbtacks in her one hand. She had a corkboard covered with photos from the case, but it was all blurring together. She'd been at it for three hours now, trying to see the connections, trying to keep her brain working on the puzzle and not thinking about Stewart and the way he'd kissed her today in the car.

She put down the box of thumbtacks and rubbed a hand over her eyes. She missed him. How many evenings had she worked away on a case while Stew went home to maintain some balance in his life? This wasn't anything different. Except this time, she wasn't sure how long he'd remain her partner.

And she couldn't blame him for this, or even herself. This connection between them had been steadily growing over the last three years, and at some point their bond had crossed that line between professional and more, and neither of them had even realized it. But sitting here in her office alone, she missed him desperately, and she knew why.

It was because she'd fallen in love with him. He wasn't the only one, but she could also see their future together easily enough. She'd disappoint him, and in turn, he'd break her heart. Because look at them— he was at home, sorting out his issues in an emotionally healthy way, and she was at work. They were opposites who complimented each other on a case, but who could never count on these deep feelings between them to sustain a real life relationship.

Or could they? That was the problem. She had no idea. All she'd ever seen in her family were people who'd loved each other and hadn't been able to make a marriage last. But that wasn't a problem she was going to sort out tonight, either.

Penny pushed herself to her feet and headed over to the corkboard again. Nothing was changing. Maybe she should just get a taxi and go home.

She glanced down at a little pile of local newspapers. She liked to stay current with local news—it was invaluable in investigations, although she doubted the gentle stories of the last week would shed any light on a cold case from five decades ago, but she liked to keep up-to-date with them all the same.

Penny picked up the first newspaper and flipped it open. It had very little of interest inside, and she put it aside, picking up the second. This paper was a little thicker, and in the center of it, after a Daily Smile page that featured a local person smiling and answering a few questions, there were the Personal Announcements. She scanned down a list of baby announcements, and her gaze stopped at a black-and-white wedding photo featuring a curly haired bride and her proud groom. But it wasn't the couple that caught her eye—it was the bride's jewelry.

An ornate necklace hung around her neck with one rather large ruby in the center, and Penny had seen that necklace before. Her gaze whipped over to her corkboard, and then back to the grainy black-and-white photo. If this wasn't the same necklace, it was an awfully close reproduction! If she'd gone through these papers earlier, she would have seen the clue staring her in the face, although she didn't know about the jewelry until recently. She whispered a silent prayer of thanks for the timing.

The bride's name was Bridget Browne who'd recently married Nate Browne on the steps of the old courthouse. Bridget was the daughter of Ernest and Anne Miller. A relative of Mike Miller's, she wondered?

This was a break—she glanced at her phone—at nine thirty at night. Her first instinct was to call Stewart and tell him what she'd discovered, but he'd said he needed some time, and he'd back in the morning.

It was too late to go knocking on the doors of newlyweds, too. This could wait until morning.

Yesterday, she would have at least sent him a text, and her finger hovered over her phone. What would she have said? Something like, "I found something! Are you glad you have a workaholic partner now?" And he'd have called right back and asked her what she'd had for dinner. She'd tell him about the trash she ate, and he'd joke about making a proper steak. Always joking…but he would have meant it. He actually cared about whether or not she ate properly, and she privately enjoyed that he cared.

But instead she stood there alone in her office, a lead in hand and her heart welling up with sadness. She had to swallow against the lump rising in her throat.

Her phone rang—it was Stewart, and she couldn't help the smile as she picked up his call.

"My SUV got vandalized," Stewart said. "I just want you to know that you don't need to bother with it. I'm getting some officers to take the report, and I'll bring it into the garage to get it fixed first thing in the morning."

"Someone targeting you this time?" she asked. "What do you mean 'don't bother with it'? Are we partners or not?"

"I'm saying, it's fine. I've got it handled," he said. "Get some rest tonight, Pen."

Things weren't going to go back to normal between her and Stew, were they?

Late the next morning after he'd dropped his SUV off at the dealership and picked up a loaner vehicle, Stewart stood in Penny's office, the two photos in his hands, scanning both photos for some discrepancy.

Penny looked less rested than usual this morning, some faint rings under her eyes like she hadn't slept properly. He'd been tempted to pick up a bagel for her on his way to the station, but he'd stopped himself. That wasn't how work professionals treated each other. She'd have to sort out her own blood sugar this morning, because it wasn't really his business, was it?

He'd brought her a coffee, though. He hadn't been able to stop himself from doing that much. As long as she was his partner, there had to be some perk, didn't there?

The two necklaces looked like an exact match to him, and he lifted his gaze to meet Penny's. A smile hovered on her lips.

"What do you think?" Penny asked, and his heart gave a tumble. Letting go of these feelings for Penny was going to be incredibly difficult.

"It looks like a pretty close match to me," he replied. "Let's go have a chat with the new Mr. and Mrs. Browne. Maybe they'll

be able to shed some light on that necklace."

Had it been stolen? Purchased? Or was it
just a good fake? Maybe when they saw it
up close, they'd see that it wasn't a match
at all. They'd find out.

Penny drove their shared cruiser to the
address they'd sussed out for the newly
married couple. Hopefully one of them
would be home, but he wanted to get a
feeling for their environment. There was a
certain amount a detective could see showing up unannounced that would be hidden
away if they gave any notice.

As they drove, they discussed the questions they wanted to ask the young woman
so that they'd be on the same page if she
was available for questioning, but there
was something about their banter today
that felt leaden. The spark had seeped out
of their partnership, and was replaced with
a deep sadness inside of him. There had
been a thrill about walking that edge with
Penny, but now that they'd faced it, he'd

discovered exactly what he'd stood to lose. Everything.

The couple lived in a duplex on a quiet, new cul-de-sac. The trees on this street were all small and supported by stakes and wires to help them grow straight. Obviously a very new area. They parked along the street, then walked up to the front door and knocked.

A dog barked from inside, and the door opened to reveal a plump young woman in workout clothes, her hair pulled up in a messy bun. Stewart recognized her from the wedding photo.

"Hi, are you Bridget Browne?" Penny asked with a smile, and she showed her badge.

"Yes. Is there a problem?" Bridget's gaze flickered between them uncertainly.

"There is no emergency," Penny said. "Don't worry about that. We're looking into an old case, and we were hoping we could ask you a few questions."

Bridget exhaled a breath of relief. "Yeah,

sure. Come in. I was just doing some yoga, but that can wait."

Bridget opened the door and let them inside. The duplex was cozy and small, but it was neatly furnished and had a couple of framed wedding photos on the wall. There was a yoga mat on the floor, and Bridget retrieved it and rolled it up.

"Can I get you some tea or something?" Bridget asked.

"This won't take long," Stewart said.

Penny settled on the couch, and Bridget sat down opposite her on an easy chair. Stewart stood behind Penny and tried to look casual.

"First of all, congratulations on your wedding," Penny said. "How long have you been married now?"

Stewart listened to the banter that Penny kept flowing. How long they'd been married—two months now. How the couple met—in high school. How big the wedding had been—a few hundred people.

"I have a lot of family around here," Bridget said.

"What's your maiden name?" Penny asked brightly.

"Miller."

"As in… Mike Miller, who used to own the hotel in town?" Penny asked artlessly. She was good, Stewart had to give her that.

"Yeah, he's my grandpa," Bridget said. "He knows absolutely everyone. He's a pillar of the community, so when I got married I had to invite just about everyone."

"I can understand that," Penny said with a smile. "I actually noticed your picture in the paper. That was a beautiful dress."

"Thank you." Bridget's face colored. "The dress was actually my mom's, and we used the same fabric and lace to have it redone for me. So it looks really different than it did when my mother wore it, but it's still really special."

"That necklace was really pretty," Penny said. "Was it hers, too?"

"No, not my mom's. That's from my

dad's side of the family," Bridget said, and he could see her opening up, relaxing. "It's been in the family for generations. My grandfather gave it to me before we got married."

"It's an antique?" Penny asked.

"Oh yes."

"And when did your family come by it?"

"I don't know," Bridget said. "Somehow, someone got it, and it just kept getting passed down."

"Who gave it to your grandfather?" Penny asked.

"His mother. It was a way to pass along family wealth, he said. And she wanted him to have it. My grandpa told me to hold on to it and sell it if we ever needed extra money. But I'd never sell a family heirloom!"

He suggested she sell a family heirloom? People didn't do that, but they might suggest selling a stolen necklace.

"I'm surprised your grandfather didn't

give it to your parents," Stewart said. "Or one of his other children."

"My dad actually never knew about it. That necklace was a well-kept secret," Bridget replied. "Grandpa gave it to me just before my wedding, and no one knew anything about it before! In fact, everyone thought it was costume jewelry when they saw me on my wedding day."

"But it's not?" Stewart asked.

"It's real." She lowered her voice. "I brought it by a jewelry store, and they took a look at the stones. They said it's worth a fortune."

This was it—Stewart could feel it. They'd stumbled across the stolen necklace that connected with the earring found at the bottom of that well.

Bridget's gaze flickered between them. "Is there a problem with the necklace?"

"It matches a description we were given, that's all," Penny said. "Do you think we could take a look at it?"

"It's not here at the house," Bridget said.

"We keep it in a safe deposit box at the bank. Once we found out how much it was worth, we didn't want to risk it."

"Well, that's smart," Penny said. "If we need to take a closer look, we'll come back with a warrant, but we really appreciate you taking the time to chat with us today."

Bridget turned a little pale, but she nodded. "Okay…"

Penny stood up and they headed back to the door.

"Thanks again," Penny said. And she pulled out a business card. "If you want to get in touch with me for any reason, this is my contact information."

Bridget accepted the card woodenly. "Can you just tell me if there's something wrong with the necklace?"

"We're just looking into it," Penny assured her. "Try not to worry about it."

When they were back in the cruiser again, Stewart got behind the wheel this time, and Penny pulled out her phone to make notes.

"If that's our stolen necklace, then it came from Mike Miller," Stewart said. "But we aren't getting a warrant to pick it up without more proof than two grainy photographs."

"True." Penny looked toward the duplex, and Stewart spotted Bridget staring out the window at them. She quickly stepped back when she saw them returning her gaze. "And we don't have much time before Bridget calls her grandfather, or goes down to Shady Oaks to talk to him in person."

"We'd better beat her there, then," Stewart said, and he put the cruiser into gear. "Let's go have another chat with Mike Miller and see where he really got that necklace. Because I'm pretty confident his dearly departed mother did not slip him an expensive set of jewelry on her deathbed unbeknownst to anyone else in the family. That's the shakiest story I've heard in a really long time."

Mike had been best friends with Caleb… Had Caleb given it to him to hold on to? Or had Mike and Caleb worked together in robbing their friend? Either way, these were not good men.

When they arrived at the Shady Oaks Retirement Lodge, the nurse at the desk was less accommodating than at their first visit.

"Mr. Miller was quite upset last time, and we notified his son about you questioning him. His son says he can't talk to you without a lawyer."

"Is his son his power of attorney?" Stewart asked.

"No."

"Then we'll need to hear Mr. Miller tell us he wants his attorney present," Stewart replied. "And we need to speak with him."

The nurse immediately began dialing, and she eyed the officers as she began speaking quickly into the receiver.

"Mr. Miller? Those officers are here to

talk with your father again. I have no legal reason to stop them, so if you want to be here, I suggest you get over here now. I'm bringing them to talk to him now."

She clicked off and gave them a nod.

"Follow me, please."

They were ushered down a hallway toward Mike Miller's room. The nurse knocked on his door, and a moment later, the old man opened it. He blinked at them for a moment, and Stewart thought he saw a flicker of fear in the old man's eyes.

"So you're back," Mike said.

"Yes, sir," Penny said. "We just have a couple of follow-up questions, if you have the time."

"Would you like an attorney present, Mr. Miller?" the nurse asked.

Penny flashed him a smile. Stewart knew just how disarming her smile could be, but he didn't think it was Penny's demeanor that made Mike step back and hold his room door open. He looked tired.

"You might as well come inside and ask

your questions," Mike said, and he turned toward the nurse. "Call my son. I don't have a lawyer, but get him down here. In the meantime, could we have some privacy, please?"

"I've already called him. He's on his way," she replied with a concerned frown. "I can stay until he arrives."

"No," Mike replied. "This is fine."

The nurse left and Mike let the door fall shut. Then he hobbled over to his walker and sat down on the little seat it provided.

"Ask away," Mike said.

"Your granddaughter's necklace from her wedding day," Penny said. "Where did it come from?"

Mike licked his lips, and for a moment, he sat in silence. Then he sighed.

"I shouldn't have given it to her... I told her not to wear it. I told her to just tuck it away, but she loved the connection to my mother, and..."

The old man rubbed a hand over his chin. Lying was hard work, and Mike was looking defeated now. Maybe he was ready to come clean.

"Is it really connected to your mother?" Stewart asked quietly.

"Of course. It was a gift on her death-bed."

"Or is it possibly connected to your best friend, Caleb Renno?" Penny asked.

Mike's gaze flicked up. "What?"

"The matching earring was discovered in the well," Stewart said. "We know about the stolen jewelry set."

Mike's chin trembled. "What…?"

"Yes, in the well, with Caleb's body."

Mike nodded slowly, pursed his lips, and after a moment he said, "I need my son."

"He's on his way. Do you want your son to hear everything?"

"It was a long time ago! Why won't you let this go?" Mike erupted.

There was someone else demanding that they do the same thing, and the only name they had connected to it was a Bryce Miller who had that string of petty charges against his name… Miller—a popular name in these parts, but also the same name as Mike Miller.

"Who is Bryce?" Stewart asked.

"You leave my grandson out of this!" Mike lifted a shaky finger. "He's getting his act together, and he'll be just fine. If you're threatening him, I will use every last penny I own to hire lawyers to fight you! I will—"

The bedroom door flung open and a portly man in his early fifties barged into the room.

"Leave my father alone!" he barked. "What do you think you're doing, badgering an old man? You are not to speak with him without me present!"

"You have no legal right to demand that," Stewart replied calmly. "What's your name?"

"Ernie Miller, and I'm his son. Dad— stop talking. Don't say another word. I'm finding you a lawyer."

Lawyering up pretty fast.

"So who is Bryce—your son?" Penny asked, turning on Ernie and fixing him with a steely gaze.

"Bryce? What's happened?"

"I'm asking about a family relationship," Penny said briskly. "Is he your son?"

"Yes, he's my oldest son. Why? What's going on?"

"And your daughter would be Bridget Miller Browne, newly married?" Penny asked.

"Yes! What is going on here?"

"Okay…" Penny shrugged. "We're looking into a missing jewelry set that's worth a small fortune. If you're so sure that your father is innocent, then I suppose your daughter must be the liar. You should know she was trying to pin the whole thing on you, Mike. She said you gave her that necklace for her wedding day."

"What—" Ernie paled. "Leave my daughter alone."

"We have to follow the clues, sir," Stewart said. "And they are leading straight to her."

Mike shut his eyes and exhaled a slow breath. "I shouldn't have done it… It was just so tempting."

"Dad!" And suddenly, Ernie reached behind him whipped out a gun. "Everyone just stop talking!"

The room silenced, and Stewart's gaze flickered between the gun held in the man's white-knuckled grip and his twitching face.

"What are you doing, Ernie?" Stewart asked quietly.

"Ernie, don't do that—" Mike said at the same time.

"Dad—just stop! Don't say another word! I told you, we need a lawyer!"

"Well, you do now…" Penny muttered.

"Shut up!" Ernie's voice was rising. "I need to think!"

"It's me or my granddaughter," Mike said. "You think this is the answer, Ernie? You can't save us all." He turned toward

Stewart and Penny. "There was Aaron Gelesky with this old set of jewelry that he
had no idea what to do with, and my hotel
was really suffering back then. No one
was visiting our neck of the woods with
all the newer hotels around, and I was sink-
ing under a heavy mortgage. The financial
strain was terrible. I was hardly sleeping
at night, and I was trying to hide the worst
of it from my wife and the kids."

Ernie's hand was shaking now, and Stewart reached out and snatched the gun out of
the man's trembling grip. He put the safety
on and Penny grabbed his arm and twisted
it hard, whipping out her cuffs at the same
time.

"You're going to have to sit tight, but best
believe you'll be facing some charges,"
Penny said.

"The cuffs are too tight," Ernie said.

"Then, don't struggle," she said curtly.

"Ernie, you're getting yourself into trouble," Mike said, shaking his head. "A gun?

Officers, please, let my son go. I'll tell you everything."

"We're detectives, and that's not going to happen. Who stole the necklace and earrings?" Stewart asked quietly.

Caleb—that's what Stewart was expecting to hear.

Mike's gaze flickered between Ernie, whose shoulders were now hunched in defeat, and Stewart. "It was easy. I cut one wire, broke a window and walked right in. I knew where it was kept, got it and walked back out. No one saw anything except… It was really early in the morning, and I still to this day have no idea what Caleb Renno was doing out there on the street! But there he was, staring at me in shock. I just walked past him and went back to the hotel. He never mentioned it to me. Never brought it up. Never asked me a question."

It wasn't Caleb! That would have been an easy lie to sell, too, but it looked like Mike was tired of dancing around untruths.

"Dad—" Ernie said, his voice shaking.

"I'm old, Ernie," Mike said. "And I'll have to meet my Maker sooner than later."

"What did you do with the jewelry?" Stewart asked.

"I brought it home and hid it my own closet. I know, real original. But then I had the problem of trying to sell it. And I was terrified that Caleb would say something to someone, get me thrown in jail."

"So you went to see him that night…" Penny prompted.

"Yeah." He nodded slowly. "It had been a few months. I needed to unload the jewelry. There was no point in having it if I couldn't sell it and lighten a few of my own debts. I wanted to both make sure he'd keep his mouth shut, and I wanted to help him out, too. They'd been having tough times financially as well, and I figured we could both benefit. I brought one of the earrings. I met him outside and had him walk into the woods with me a bit. I didn't want to risk anyone else seeing the jewels.

I showed him the earring and told him he could take it apart and sell the jewels separately. That way they couldn't be traced, and no one would be the wiser. But his money problems would be over."

"What went wrong?" Stewart asked.

Ernie sank down to a chair, resting his face in his hands.

"He was offended," Mike said softly. "He was furious that I'd try to include him in my crime. He said I needed to get off his property and never speak to him again. I don't know who threw the first punch, but…we started fighting and I got hold of a rock. I swung…" The old man shut his eyes. "I killed my best friend…and when I realized he was dead, I saw the old well, and I dumped him down there. I didn't know the earring went with him. I looked around for it, I couldn't find it, and I just covered up the well again and got out of there."

Stewart could feel the heaviness of the room around them, and he looked over at

Penny to see her eyes misting with unshed tears.

"What about the story of the car that took Caleb away?" Stewart asked.

"I made it up. I had to make people believe he'd left. I told a couple of people. The rumor spread. Everyone loves to blame an outsider."

"But you came back to Elizabeth and brought her groceries and other things she needed," Penny said, her voice choked.

"I was plagued with guilt!" Mike said. "I'd killed her husband! It wasn't on purpose, but I'd done it. And I couldn't let anyone know he was dead, or I'd end up in prison. I had a family who needed me, too. So I did my best by her, I tried to make up for what I'd done. I knew it wouldn't, but I truly was sorry! I had nightmares for years. I still do sometimes. But it was something in the heat of the moment. I didn't really mean to kill him. I just…swung!"

"Did your wife know?" Penny asked.

Mike shook his head. "My wife was innocent. She was a good woman with a big heart. She just thought I was being kind to my best friend's widow. She didn't like it, though. She thought it was weird and that I should focus on her, not Elizabeth. She died never knowing why."

Another woman who probably thought she wasn't loved—that was ironic.

"And your son?" Stewart asked.

Ernie just looked up, his face filled with misery. Yeah, Ernie knew already. And they'd passed the necklace on to his daughter. So whatever remorse they'd felt about that murder hadn't been strong enough to make them let go of the jewelry.

"You let Elizabeth believe that Caleb left her," Penny said. "You let her think he'd stopped loving her."

Mike was silent and his lips trembled.

"I think you were right about your father needing a lawyer," Stewart said quietly to Ernie.

Mike looked up at him, squinting. "Just

leave my granddaughter out of it. She had no idea."

"What about Bryce?" Penny asked.

"My son was just trying to protect his grandfather!" Ernie started to stand, then sank back into the chair.

"By following police officers, issuing threats and vandalizing private property?" Stewart asked. They might not have the proof yet, but he had a feeling that they'd all crumble under questioning. Mike already had, and that was the start. Yeah, they'd be charged, too.

"Are we ready?" Stewart asked.

Penny nodded mutely.

"Michael Miller, you are under arrest for robbery and for the murder of Caleb Renno. You have the right to remain silent. Anything you say can and will be used against you in the court of law. You have the right to an attorney..."

Stewart could say the words without even thinking, and as he officially arrested

338   *Grave Amish Secrets*

the elderly man, Stewart couldn't help but think that the most damaging thing Mike Miller had done hadn't been the robbery or even the murder…it had been the insidious suggestion that Caleb had stopped loving his family.

Mike held out his wrists for cuffs, but those wouldn't be necessary. Stewart put a hand under Mike's arm and helped him rise to his feet.

Stewart and Penny would get Mike a wheelchair and bring him down to the station where he'd be charged with robbery and second-degree murder. Ernie would be charged with aggravated assault of a law enforcement officer because of the gun brandishing. Once charges were laid, Mike would likely stay in this very retirement home with an ankle monitor while he waited for his trial date. His son would get a jail cell.

The man who'd killed his best friend was gone. And the elderly version of him who remained was a frail shell who'd lived with the guilt of his crimes for nearly fifty years.

"Do you have anything you want to say to him before we bring him into the station?" Stewart asked Penny.

Penny's lips were nearly white.

"Yes," she said softly. "I do."

Mike looked up at her, his blue eyes watery.

"*Mammi* thought her husband stopped loving her... You killed more than a good man, Mike. You killed her belief that her love meant anything, and that bled out into the rest of us. And you watched that happen. You might be sorry for what you did, but you watched Elizabeth's family struggle on a heart level, and your confession would have spared generations of pain! So don't look for any compassion from me. You had forty-eight years to make this right. Forty-eight years!" She swallowed hard then, and headed for the door. "I'll call it in, Stew."

Stewart nodded. She'd said what she needed to say.

TWELVE

That evening, Penny and her mother sat in *Mammi*'s Amish kitchen, mugs of hot tea in front of them. Sarah had brought along a large bucket of Kentucky Fried Chicken, fries, and coleslaw, although none of them were particularly hungry. Sarah had picked up some knitting needles for the first time in decades and was trying her hand at the craft.

"You still knit like you're butchering a hog," Elizabeth said with a low laugh.

"I haven't done this since I was a teenager," Sarah chuckled.

"It's nice to see you trying again," Elizabeth replied.

The needles clicked as Sarah knitted stitch after stitch. It was slow, but Sarah was making progress. Penny had never in her life seen her mother doing a handcraft, and it was almost like watching her own mother move back in time, back to when everything was different, and Sarah had known how to knit.

They'd been over the facts of the case again and again—all three of them seeming to need the repetition to make it all sink in.

"Mike Miller..." Sarah murmured for the hundredth time as she focused on the moving needles. "He visited us! He sat at this very table. He gave us kids advice, and he paid our bills sometimes."

"It was guilt," Penny said. "He knew what he'd done, and he was trying to fix it."

"So it was an impulsive crime," Sarah said. "He hadn't planned it..."

"No, but he still killed your father," Penny replied. He'd lied to a whole family for years. He'd led them to believe their father hadn't loved them enough to stay—that a man's love couldn't be trusted.

"Did he seem remorseful now?" Sarah asked.

Penny thought back to the old man's tear-filled eyes. He was so very sorry, he kept repeating. So very sorry... Had he lived through enough punishment already, or had he managed to escape it? That was the question that only God above could answer.

"Very remorseful," Penny said bitterly. "For whatever that's worth. His son was willing to shoot us to keep the secret, though. And his grandson is a real piece of work."

More generational trauma that had bled down from father to son to grandson...

"It's worth a great deal," Elizabeth said, rousing herself. "To *Gott*, it matters. When we repent, He is faithful and just to forgive us."

"*Mammi*, we're talking about our feelings, not theological facts," Penny said.

"My feelings matter significantly less than the Word of *Gott*," Elizabeth replied. "And we are told that if we want to be forgiven, we must forgive. That's a theological fact, too."

"I know, *Mamm*," Sarah said, finishing a row and setting her little strip of knitting aside. "And you will forgive, I know you will. But right now, what are you feeling?"

Tears welled in Elizabeth's eyes. "I'm feeling guilty!"

"For what?" Sarah asked, reaching across the table to grasp her mother's hand. "You did nothing wrong!"

"I did… I allowed myself to enjoy a man's feelings for me. I was proper—I didn't allow anything untoward…but when Mike's wife had passed away, I allowed myself to feel tender feelings for Mike Miller. I told myself it was just a special friendship, but I was enjoying his company, too. I didn't say a word. I didn't cross lines, but I did enjoy his company…"

"*Mamm*, you didn't know!" Sarah said.

"He killed my Caleb!" Elizabeth whispered and she wiped a tear from her cheek. "And I remembered everything through the lens of Caleb leaving me. I looked back on happy days and remembered them less happily because I thought Caleb left. I remembered his weaknesses bitterly. I interpreted his actions differently... I wasn't fair to poor Caleb. He'd loved us after all."

"*Mammi*," Penny said. "Those were lies, and now you know differently. Now you can remember him properly."

"Believing my father left us changed everything for me," Sarah said. "My therapist pointed out that I treat men like they'll leave until they do." She looked over at Penny. "And I've passed that fear on to you, too."

"I don't think so," Penny murmured.

"Oh, I do," Sarah replied. "You've done the same thing I have—you push men away before they have a chance to hurt you."

"All of you *kinner* left the faith," Elizabeth said. "If you couldn't trust your own father, then how could you trust the faith he raised you to?"

"That's true," Sarah replied. "It's why I left. I hated him. I hated that he'd abandoned us, and I was going to find a life I could actually trust."

"I'm still in church," Penny said.

"Thank the Lord for that," Sarah murmured. "But we all three of us have to admit that believing my father left shaped us. It changed us. It changed our view of the world, and our view of love."

"Yes, I think that's true," Penny said softly. She'd lived her life afraid of being rejected like her sweet grandmother had been, like her spunky mother had been… Worthy women had their hearts broken all the time, especially in their family.

Penny had seen the world through a certain lens, too. She saw the marriages that ended, not the ones that lasted. She'd seen the incompatibilities, not the ties that bound two people together. She lived her life waiting for the inevitable end to a loving relationship because she thought she was being realistic.

But somewhere she'd read that the ugly, dirty street was just as real as the morning mist that swirled so beautifully above it. Maybe she'd missed some beauty over the years because she'd been so focused on the dirty street.

"What makes a marriage last?" Sarah asked softly.

Penny and her mother would both have to reevaluate their lives, their choices, their fears and even their hopes. Because Penny wanted the kind love that kept a man coming home to her day after day, year after year, and only death itself could part them.

"What makes a marriage last? It's love and a willingness to bend," Elizabeth replied. "It's what I've seen in the marriages around me—my parents, my siblings, my neighbors and friends... While I was busy wondering how I'd gone wrong in my own marriage, I was watching."

"I wonder if there's still hope for me," Sarah said.

"I think so," Penny said. "Mom, you're a beautiful, smart woman. Of course you can find love again. And maybe you'll have more clarity this time. Maybe we all will in this family."

"Even you?" Sarah asked meaningfully.

Penny looked toward the window at the lowering sun. Her heart was filled to the brim with one man whom she'd been so afraid to love. Because what if he left her? What if she lost him completely? What if he broke her heart?

Her grandmother stood up from the table and went over to the sink. She stood there, looking out the window, her expression filled with forlorn sadness.

"What about me?" Penny deflected with a short laugh.

"What about Stew?" Sarah asked softly.

Penny swallowed hard. What about him, indeed? There was one thing she knew for sure. "He loves me."

"And you love him," Sarah said matter-of-factly. "I know you well enough to see when you're head over heels for a man, and Stewart Jones has been your platonic other half. What's been holding you back from making that romantic?"

"Fear." It was plain and simple.

"Is that all?"

"It's enough, isn't it?" Penny asked.

"Sweetie," Sarah said quietly, "finding out about my father's dedication to us changes things. My father didn't leave us. He didn't stop loving us. It took his *murder* to keep him away. As your mother, I wanted to keep you safe, to keep you vigilant and careful…but there's a point where a woman can be so careful that she ends up alone anyway. I'm walking proof of that."

"Mom, you're not alone. You have me."

"I'm not complaining," Sarah said. "And I'm not exactly giving up on myself, either. But I'm looking at my daughter in love with a good man, and I don't want you to make the mistakes I did."

"It's more complicated than that. I'm not what Stew needs," Penny said, tears rising in her eyes. "He needs a woman who's outside of our job, who can give him the peace and tranquility that will comfort him. I'm too close to all of it, and I deal with things by throwing myself into it even more. You don't understand—he loves me, yes, but I'm not what he needs."

"I saw the way he looked at you," Sarah said. "I have a feeling you're exactly what he needs."

Sarah picked up her knitting again and stabbed a needle through the strings of yarn with a squeak because the stitches were so tight.

"My Caleb loves me," Elizabeth murmured, her gaze trained out the window. "I wonder when he'll be home?"

Sarah and Penny exchanged a look. *Mammi*'s mind was wandering again, but at least it was back at a happier time.

"*Mamm*, you're getting confused," Sarah said, raising her voice.

"Oh, let her be," Penny said. "It's her mind's way of remembering, I think. And now she can remember him as he really was."

"On his way home," Sarah said, blinking back tears.

Elizabeth looked back at the table, her gaze landing on Sarah's knitting.

"No, no, Sarah," Elizabeth said, and bustled over to where Sarah sat. "You're clutching it all so tightly. You're knitting it into a knot. You've got to grip it gently, like you're holding a dove in your hands. Don't squeeze, and don't pull, just loop, and bring it through, loop, and bring it through..." Elizabeth's veined and wrinkled hands covered Sarah's fingers. "Gently. Loosely. Trust the process. Loop, and bring it through. Yes, see? Do you see the difference?"

And suddenly, as Penny watched her grandmother giving her middle-aged mother a knitting lesson, the deeper truth of her words suddenly shone out like the last rays of that setting sun.

Hold it gently. Lovingly. Trust the process...

Penny had been holding on to her life with a death grip, trying to keep everything in place lest she find herself heartbroken. But that wasn't the secret, was it? In her mind's eye, she saw Stewart with one of his special little smiles, holding out a coffee to her and asking what she'd eaten recently, and she felt such a wave of longing for him that tears sprung to her eyes.

She was suddenly seeing a different way of approaching life—the way she might have approached things if Caleb had never been killed and the family had never been scarred by lies...

Lord, she prayed silently, *can I trust Stewart with my heart? Because I think I want to try.*

Normally, Stewart went home earlier in the evening than this, but tonight he found himself in his office, staring at his neat, sparse furnishings, and wondering if maybe he was a little too sparing with his heart in this job.

It had been a busy day and now a busy evening. They'd picked up Bryce at his home, and Ernie and Bryce had both crumbled under questioning. Bryce was trying to protect his family in the only belligerent way he knew. Ernie had known all along that necklace was stolen, and he'd been determined to protect his father and the jewels, which he seemed to think were worth even more than they were. There were a lot of charges being laid—the more serious being those against Mike Miller for murder. The chief had just shaken his head in disbelief.

"I remember Mr. Miller from the Christmas Toy Drive the Little Dusseldorf church put on," he'd said. "I remember him giving more generously than anyone else to the food bank... Mr. Miller?"

But some people overcompensated for

their crimes. Mr. Miller had been doing all of those things to try and make up for some very serious criminal actions. And he'd confessed.

So Stewart sat here in his office, his heart wrapped up in a knot, and all he could seem to do was pray that God in his mercy and justice would sort all of this out according to His will. Because who was Stewart but a detective looking for the truth? And the truth of a crime wasn't always the whole truth of a story. The subtleties and nuances would have to be entrusted to a jury.

Stewart pushed himself to his feet and headed out of his office and down the hall. Penny's office door was closed, and he paused at the nameplate, his heart tugging toward it. Not so long ago, she would have been at work late, too, and something inside of him was so drawn to that messy, disorganized, overflowing office.

But he knew why he'd stayed at work tonight. It was because it felt closer to her. Going home felt like shutting a door. Staying late? This felt like possibility still, and his heart wasn't ready to quit.

Funny how his safe, orderly home wasn't comforting right now. When his heart was in a tangle, he wasn't yearning for those proper boundaries and the tranquility of turning off his cell phone. What he wanted was Penny.

He headed over to the water cooler and filled a little plastic cup with water that was too cold to drink. He sipped at it. A couple of troopers were at their desks in the bullpen, typing away on their keyboards.

This was foolish. He should go.

"Hey, Stew?" Nick Adams sat at his desk with a form in front of him.

"Hey, Nick," Stewart said, walking over to the other investigator's desk.

"I, uh—" Nick looked up, his face coloring a little bit. "I have something personal I'm doing, and I was wondering if I could count on both your advice and your discretion."

"Of course." Stewart pulled up a chair and sat down. "You got it. How can I help?"

"I'm going for couple's counseling with my wife, and the therapist gave us some homework," he said, his voice low.

"Like…going home at a decent time?" Stewart asked wryly.

"Among other things," Nick said with a low laugh. "No, this was something she asked me to ask some coworkers about."

"Okay," Stewart sobered.

"She says I need to find a way to process everything we see here so that when I'm at home, I can be fully present," Nick said. "And you seem to have the best work-life boundaries of anyone. How do you do it?"

"I—" Stewart felt the air seep out of his lungs. "I'm not as good at it as I thought I was, honestly. I kept a really firm line between work and home, and tried to keep the bad stuff out. But I've realized recently that it isn't working."

"Oh." Nick sighed. "That's not what I was hoping to hear."

"It's not about the rigid boundaries,"

Stewart said. "I'm realizing that now. It's finding the beauty in the world. Finding it around you in unexpected places. Because you can't just focus on the cases, or you'll burn out."

His gaze moved toward Penny's closed office door. It wasn't the boundaries. It wasn't the quiet music and dim lights at his home. He suddenly knew exactly what it was that kept him grounded and seeing beauty in the world.

It wasn't a theory or an exercise. It was one woman. He came into work and saw her. He went to the coffee shop and got her order. He made dinner and he thought about what he could do to make sure she got some of the good stuff he enjoyed. They went over a case, and he looked up in the sparkling, beautiful eyes of his partner…

His boundaries hadn't been protecting his balance—she had been.

"Go home, Nick," Stewart said. "And when you get there, look into your wife's eyes and remember why you married her.

Text her during the day. Pick up little treats for her on your way home. Make her your touchstone, and I think you'll be okay. The cases will be here tomorrow."

Nick blinked. "Um...okay." He was still for a second, then started gathering up his papers and filing them away. "You're right. I'm going home."

Stewart would do the same thing—he'd head home—but he wasn't quite so blessed as Nick was. He wasn't going home to the woman who balanced out his world.

The station front door opened, and his heart stuttered when he saw Penny. Her hair was loose around her shoulders, and her makeup had long since worn off. She looked tired, but still so pretty. She hesitated when she spotted him and their gazes met in an electric clash. What were they going to do—step around each other for next few months?

"Penny!" His voice was louder than it should have been, and he felt some heat touch his face. "Could I discuss something with you? In my office?"

Penny looked startled, but she nodded, and Stewart gave Nick's desk a tap in farewell and headed into his office. Penny followed him inside, and he swung the door shut with a solid bang. She shot him a look of surprise.

"What's going on?" she asked.

That was when Stewart pulled her into his arms, then lowered his lips over hers. Her eyes fluttered shut and he kissed her with all the pent-up longing that he'd been trying to ignore for far too long. When he pulled back, he felt like another part of him had finally clicked into place.

"Okay, here's the thing," he said, his arms still around her. "I love you. And you think I need someone different, but I don't. Do you know what keeps me seeing the beauty in the world? You do. Do you know what keeps me grounded? You. What reminds me of a happy future? You again. I know I thought I needed a different kind of woman to keep me balanced, but you're the one who's done that for me all this time. I just didn't realize it. I love you. I don't want anyone else, and I know you're going through a lot right now, and you probably have a lot of stuff to process, and—"

"I realized something today watching my mother knit," Penny said, with a smile tickling her lips. "I don't know if I could even put it into words, but long story short, if there is one man whose heart I can trust, it's yours. But I need to know one thing."

"Okay?" Stewart said.

"Will you ever stop loving me?" She looked up at him earnestly.

"Nope," he replied without missing a beat.

"I'm being serious. I want you to think about it."

"So am I," he replied. "And I don't need to think about it. I love you, and if you'll let me, I'll just keep on loving you. It's the way I'm wired, Pen. You know me well enough, don't you?"

She nodded. "I suppose I do."

"So…do you think we could go out tonight and talk? Maybe we can get some ice cream or something."

"I just had half a bucket of KFC," she said with a rueful smile.

"So…a green smoothie?" he asked with a laugh. "Where are we landing here?"

"How about just a cup of herbal tea?" she asked, and her eyes softened as her gaze met his. "And maybe on Sundays we could start going to church together, too."

Stewart pressed a kiss against her forehead, closing his eyes and inhaling the soft scent of her shampoo and that perfume she always wore. It calmed his heart.

"Just so you know, I plan on marrying you one of these days," he murmured against her hair.

A smile split her face. "That sounds good to me."

EPILOGUE

And that little talk in his office had ended up being their engagement, because Stew never did get down on one knee, and they'd started talking about wedding plans that very night. They'd shopped for a ring the next weekend, and wedding plans started falling into place within a month.

Mammi Elizabeth had a visit from her bishop. He had dug up the records the last bishop had kept, and he'd found a signed and dated confession of faith. The bishop assured her that Caleb had joined the church because it was where God and his conscience had led him. It had been a sincere conversion. And Elizabeth stopped worrying about her late husband's past, and started thanking God for the time she'd had with him.

Mike Miller was formally charged, but his health took a quick decline shortly afterward. He died in the hospital before he ever faced a courtroom, with a chaplain at his side. The chaplain later said that the old man had passed away with the words from Psalm 51 on his lips. "'Have mercy upon me, O God, according to thy lovingkindness: according unto the multitude of thy tender mercies blot out my transgressions. Wash me throughly from mine iniquity, and cleanse me from my sin. For I acknowledge my transgressions: and my sin is ever before me...'"

Bridget Browne, Mike's granddaughter, contacted Penny with the business card she'd left her. She wanted to apologize on behalf of her family, but Penny and God had been working together on forgiving Mike. Penny had a coffee with Bridget instead, and she invited her and her husband to the wedding. It was time for some new starts, new patterns and happier futures for all of them.

Penny and Stewart got married on a brisk fall day at Stewart's church in Lancaster. Pastor Bill officiated, and Penny vowed to love and to honor Stewart for the rest of her life. The promises were deep, and she meant every word. Stewart's "I do" was quiet and firm, and those were the most beautiful words she'd heard in her life. Because she knew that Stewart's heart was hers.

Later, their photographer took photos and everyone went to the banquet hall. As Penny and Stewart headed inside the building, Stewart tugged her down a hallway, and pulled her into his arms.

"I love you, Mrs. Jones," he said, and kissed her lips.

"I love you, too," she said.

"When did you eat last?" he asked.

"Um—" Penny started to laugh. "Breakfast. Why?"

Stewart looked at his watch, then toward the door. "Because we still have a first dance, some toasts and some speeches before the meal is served, and you're hungry."

Penny put a hand over her stomach. "I guess I am. Do you have a granola bar or something?"

"I have something better."

Just then, Nick came down the hallway, a paper bag in hand. He shot them a grin.

"I rushed, Stewart," Nick said. "But there was a line up at the burger place."

Nick handed over the paper bag, and Penny's stomach grumbled as she smelled burgers and fries. Stewart passed her a burger wrapped in paper, and they leaned over a railing and munched on the food as their guests trailed in.

"You sent Nick on a fast-food run?" Penny asked.

"Hey, I make sure you eat," Stewart said. "It's what I do."

She heard the "I love you" in the words, and she realized that every time Stewart showed up with food for the rest of their lives, she'd know it was his way of showing how much he cared. And as she chewed that delicious burger, her arm pressed against his suit, she knew that whatever they faced, they'd be just fine. They were in God's hands, and they were together.

The rest of their lives together was going to be so very sweet!

* * * * *

Dear Reader,

I hope you enjoyed this story! I love writing Amish romances. Those close-knit communities without modern conveniences tug at my imagination. Lancaster County, where this story is set, is home to one of the oldest Amish communities in the US, spread out over many towns and boroughs. Like many authors, I have made up the names of a few towns in this area.

If you haven't discovered my books yet, I have quite a backlist. I hope you'll come check them out.

If you enjoyed this book, I hope you'll leave a review. Reviews get the word out to other readers, and that helps me out a lot! If you want to thank an author for her hard work, leave a review. We just love it!

If you'd like to connect with me, you can find me at my website, patriciajohns.com, or on social media. I'd also encourage you to sign up for my newsletter, where I hold monthly giveaways. It's a great way to stay connected!

Patricia